To Maria —

We miss you Dearly
in writing group.

"PLEASE, Do Not be
Such a Stan!"

SEAN

GOING
NOWHERE
FASTER

SEAN BEAUDOIN

 LITTLE, BROWN AND COMPANY

New York ᠈᠊ Boston

Little, Brown and Company

Hachette Book Group USA
1271 Avenue of the Americas, New York, NY 10020
Visit our Web site at www.lb-teens.com

First Edition: April 2007

Library of Congress Cataloging-in-Publication Data

Beaudoin, Sean.
    Going nowhere faster / by Sean Beaudoin. — 1st ed.
       p. cm.
    Summary: Although his past accomplishments have convinced
everyone else he is headed for college and greatness, seventeen-
year-old Stan just wants to work at Happy Video, live in his parents'
basement, write a movie script — and convince someone there really
is a madman after him.
    ISBN-13: 978-0-316-01415-1
    ISBN-10: 0-316-01415-X
    [1. Creative ability — Fiction. 2. Video rental services — Fiction.
3. Self-esteem — Fiction. 4. Stalking — Fiction. 5. Family life —
Pennsylvania — Fiction. 6. Pennsylvania — Fiction.]   I. Title.
PZ7.B3805775Goi 2007
[Fic] — dc22

                                    2006027894

                              10 9 8 7 6 5 4 3 2 1

                                       QFF

                    Printed in the United States of America

For Jordan and Alec

The author wishes to thank: Alvina Ling,
Steven Malk, Christian Bauer, Cari Phillips,
Alice Jones, Lauren Tarshis, Connie Hsu, Christine Cuccio,
Kirk Benshoff, and Catherine Beaudoin
for their invaluable advice and critique during
the development of this book.

Treatment for the feature-length film titled
GOING NOWHERE FASTER©
Written by Stan Smith

Sgt. Rick Steele quits the force after his partner is killed
in a bank robbery. He starts a detective agency called Steal
Acquisitions, making a solemn vow to find the killer. Ten
years go by, but all he's done is find lost cats, follow cheating wives, and solve the mystery of a tasteless meatloaf (not
enough garlic). One morning Ginny Lambert, tall and beautiful, walks (not walks, glides) into his office. Her twin sister
has been kidnapped. (Twins? Man, oh, man.) Police are baffled.
Leads are cold. Rick, looking deep into Ginny's blue eyes,
takes the case. That night he punches information out of
various hoods and lowlifes, most of them named Maxie or
Ratso. He learns Suzie Lambert was kidnapped by a Chinese
white slavery ring. Rick and Ginny follow the trail to
Shanghai, where Ginny's sister is toiling on a collective
work farm. The foreman, in an ironed green Mao jacket, is
Scar Ramirez, the man who killed Rick's partner! Just when
they are about to free Ginny's sister, they are captured and
tortured ... and ... and ...

Oh, who the hell knows? This is terrible, isn't it?
Next thing, there's going to be a fight between Scar and Rick
on top of the Statue of Liberty. Hey, maybe that's not such a
bad idea. Actually, it is. It's a really, really terrible idea.
Never mind.

CHAPTER ONE
STRANGERS ON A *very strange and long and boring* TRAIN

My name's Stan, so right there I was more or less doomed from the beginning.

You don't think so? Try this: Close your eyes. Clear your mind. Get to a comfortable place. What does the name Stan remind you of? Football star? Lead singer? Private detective?

Nope. *Stan* is a Hollywood agent who represents anorexic twins and says "Ciao" into his cell phone all day. *Stan* is your fat uncle, the one who ruins Christmas every year never shutting up about his shoe box collection or his divorce or his acid reflux. At any rate, Stan is definitely not me, which is to say: a skinny, bored, not-worth-half-his-paycheck counter boy.

1. I work at Happy Video. (Is it really happy? Hard to tell.)
2. I wear a name tag that says: ***STAN — Head*** (also only) ***Clerk.***
3. Do you even need a number three?

As I stacked returns, a woman walked to the counter.

"Do you carry anything with Barbra Streisand?"

"No, ma'am."

"*Nothing?*"

"Sorry. Store policy."

She gave me a confused look and left. We actually do have some (*way* too many) Streisand movies, but they're all so awful I tend not to rent them. That may sound unfair, but I can tell you from experience that not a single person has ever returned *Yentl* with a smile on their face. Besides, I have other problems. Like how Chad Chilton wants to kill me. Why? He just does. On the last day of school he cornered me near the gym and said:

1. I WILL HURT YOU.

and

2. BAD.

"I've never been good at multiple choice," I said, mostly because Mr. Camacho, the Spanish teacher, was coming down the hall. Chad Chilton almost laughed, but didn't. What he did instead was poke me in the chest, hard. "Have a good summer," he said, and then walked away.

I rubbed my sternum. I decided to breathe.

"*Cómo está?*" Mr. Camacho asked, with his big smile and his tan slacks and his Estrada chin.

"Totally *bien*," I answered, and then went to my next class. That was two months ago. Now it's the middle of August and I'm still more or less intact, so maybe I lucked out. Or maybe Chad Chilton forgot. I guess it depends how optimistic you (I) want to be (not very). Twice after work I've found my bike tires slashed. I've also found notes left in my parents' mailbox: BET-TER WATCH YER ASS! And someone spray-painted STAN SMITH IS GONNAA GET IT on the sidewalk in front of Happy Video. Bad spelling is a clue even Sergeant Rick Steele couldn't miss.

"Hey, Stan!" Mr. Lawlor said, approaching the counter. "Any luck with college?"

Another problem, also sort of a minor obstacle, is that I have absolutely no chance of getting into any college, anytime, for any reason, under any circumstance, anywhere.

"No," I sighed. "No luck."

Mr. Lawlor owned a store down the street that sold (mostly didn't sell) wooden duck decoys and plastic ferns and other junk people were expected, for some reason, to put on their mantel. He slid his videos toward me, a romantic comedy on top, an action film in the middle, and, of course, something from the *Adult* section hidden beneath.

"Hey, that's too bad," he said, shifting weight, anxious for me to ring him up before a neighbor walked in and saw what was lurking below *When Harry Met Sally.* . . .

"Actually," I said, "I'm not going anywhere. I'm gonna stay in town and live in my parents' garage and write a movie script."

"Ha-ha," Mr. Lawlor laughed. "Smart kid like you?"

It had been a *really* long time since I'd won the Young Juniors' Chess Championship. My mother made me enter. The local papers took pictures of me in the world's ugliest and lamest suit and tie, and so people thought I was destined to Become

Something. What that something might be was more or less negotiable, as long as it involved a bow tie, some chalk, super-thick glasses, and lots of published articles in journals no one ever reads. What it definitely was not was my current handle as the Town's Laziest Register Monkey at the Town's Only Video Store.

"That'll be five ninety-eight, due back Wednesday."

Mr. Lawlor sweaty-palmed me a ten. I gave him change with my Blank-And-Nonjudgmental face (probably my only true clerking skill) and watched as he waddled out to his Volvo (*Spanking Professor 6* safely in the trunk) before driving the hundred yards back to Lawlor's Duck and Fern Emporium.

Okay, I made that up. That's not the name of his store. It's just called Lawlor's. But the rest is true. I'm trying hard not to exaggerate so much. For some reason, I can't help myself. My therapist says I have trouble stifling my creativity.

Dr. Felder: "You have trouble stifling your creativity."

Me: "I have trouble stifling this costs sixty an hour."

(Picture me lying on a couch. Picture Dr. Felder taking notes. Picture me rolling my eyes.)

"I sense some hostility here, Stan."

"I'm not hostile," I said. "Chad Chilton's the one who wants to kill *me*."

"Yes, I've heard that before."

"Not today."

"You're too young to be paranoid."

"Have you ever noticed that the paranoid guy is the only one who ever makes it through the night in the old cabin?"

"What old cabin?"

"The one by the haunted lake in every horror movie."

"Let's change gears for a minute." Dr. Felder sighed. "How's it coming with the lists?"

You may have noticed by now that I make lists. I can't help it. Even when I was little I made them, like my parents would come home to find me writing on the wall in orange crayon:

1. Pnut butter

2. Toy

3. Cookie

4. Ice cream

"It's coming great with the lists."

"Are you sure?"

(Cue rolling of eyes.) "Am I *sure*?"

"So tell me about rolling your eyes. What are we trying to say there?"

Anyway, the stifling creativity thing is a bunch of crap. Someone creative would've already finished their script with Bobby De Niro calling every ten minutes wanting to play the sensitive guy part. The truth is I'm a liar (serial exaggerator) and can't help it. But I'm trying to stop. I promise.

"Hey, guy!" said a freckle-face kid who leaned his BMX against the *Classics* section, knocking over a picture of Bette Davis. "You got *The Terminator?*"

(Bonus Question: Isn't renting a movie where Arnold the Austrian Meatball murders a hundred and forty-six people in the first ten minutes somehow *worse* than naked coeds?)

"No," I lied. It was clear Arnold wasn't going to do him any good.

"No?"

"No."

"This place sucks, guy," he said.

"Tell me about it."

The kid rolled his bike out the door and did a wheelie across the parking lot. A gang of other kids caught up to him, and they tore away in a pack.

In the next four hours I had eight customers, rented out three videos, and fielded five questions about college. I tried to work on my script, writing down things like *Guy goes into house. Cut to close-up. Door slams.* Great. Now what? Zombie Lacrosse Team? Ninja Rabbi? Shy Girl That Learns How To Be Beautiful in Time For The Big Dance?

No, no, and . . . uh . . . no.

I gave up and just sat behind the register and watched *In a Lonely Place,* my favorite Bogart movie. It's about a lonely guy who drives too fast and picks up women and punches people who annoy him. Perfect. I also ate potato chips and bent staples into a long chain, which looked like either raccoon DNA or the world's ugliest necklace. I was trying to decide which when Keith walked in, three hundred and twenty pounds of former football hero.

"Hey, Stan!"

He wore a ridiculous curly perm and a huge tan sweater that made him look like an offshore island.

"Hey, Keith."

He was also my boss. He was large and obviously boozy and more or less useless, but I loved him.

"What's goin' on?"

I showed him the staple necklace. I held it up to my neck and smiled like what's-his-name from Most Recent Boy Band, and in my mind girls screamed and flashbulbs went off and a white limo came roaring up at my side as a nine-foot chauffeur held the door and pushed away groupies and then whisked me over to IHOP for blintzes.

"Hey, that's beautiful," Keith said, grabbing the necklace out of my hand and tossing it into the garbage. "I'm deducting the cost of six hundred staples from your paycheck."

"I get *paid*? I thought this was volunteer."

He laughed. He gave me a wink and then opened a deluxe pack of peanut butter cups from our cardboard movie concession stand (1.15 pounds, $5.95 plus tax) and gobbled them like an Escalade topping off with diesel. His throat bulged. His ears turned pink from lack of oxygen. A customer came to the door, peeked in, then left. Keith tossed the final candy in a high arc, mouth as wide as it would go (unbelievably, amazingly, *ridiculously* wide), and missed completely. The chocolate hit him in the center of the forehead and rolled under the desk.

"So how's business?"

"Slow," I said, handing over the evening's receipts. Millville had finally gotten cable (probably the last town in America) six months ago. Everyone was at home watching infomercials or old movies with Liz Taylor where all the characters walk around in bathrobes and slippers.

"You run the numbers?"

On my first day I'd made the mistake of helping Keith when his calculator wouldn't work. (It was a solar one. It was night. He was convinced it was broken.) "Hey, Stan! Get a pencil and times me one thousand three hundred forty-five by $2.99!"

I blinked and then told him $4021.55.

He stared woozily. "How'd you do that?"

I really didn't know. Math and breathing. Breathing and math. Has anyone ever made a good movie about long division?

"Okay, smart guy, try this . . ."

He threw other numbers at me, three then four then six digits, add, subtract, multiply. I did them in my head and told him the answers. I knew math prowess was something to hide, not show off, mostly because it usually led to being punched after class, but I guess I thought Keith might give me a raise. What he did, instead, was make me start doing the books. Since his two duties as manager consisted of (1) doing the books and (2) locking up at night, this gave him plenty of time to sneak out and drink beer.

"Yeah, I ran 'em."

Keith flexed his gigantic shoulders. "My own personal genius!"

FIVE THINGS KEITH WAS BIGGER THAN:
1. Industrial boiler
2. Fish barge

3. Smallish building
4. Fattish triceratops
5. Milk truck

"Leave me alone," I said.

"Einstein with acne!"

"Shut up."

"The Michael Jordan of numbers!"

"Piss off!"

"Good idea!" he said, patting me on the shoulder and then slamming the door of the employee bathroom. An extended deluge followed. I envisioned Noah. I envisioned his ark.

"Much better," Keith said, when he finally emerged. "Now let's close this sucker down!"

I saluted and turned off the lights. He started to lower the steel gate, like he did every night, with one finger.

"Let me try."

"Go ahead."

I pulled. It wouldn't budge. I tugged and grunted. I winched and fulcrummed and levered. Finally, I just hung from the rusty bar and moved it, maybe half an inch.

"Wheaties," he advised, making a muscle.

"We're not allowed to have corporate cereal at home."

Keith winced. "No Puffs? No Pops or Smacks or Jacks or *Loops*?"

"Nope. No Loops."

He knew it wasn't a joke. My mother is six-three and vegan. She wears overalls and grows her own produce and has calloused hands and drinks gallons of carrot pulp. She's possibly the world's healthiest person. No one makes jokes about her.

"Time to run away," he advised.

"Good idea," I said, "but first I'll be needing a large raise. You know, to save up for a knapsack and a harmonica?"

Keith laughed, extra loud, like he always did when the word "raise" was used, and then got into his white Town Car (backseat full of concession candy) and peeled away. I laughed, quietly, like I always did when ending a shift at Happy Video, and then got on my white ten-speed and rolled out of the lot. Keith's headlights disappeared. I was alone. My parents' house was three miles away down a dark road, and Chad Chilton wanted to kill me.

So what else was new?

CHAPTER TWO

NAPOLEON *taking his ten-speed off some sweet jumps* **STANAMITE**

The humid air felt good on my face as I pedaled. The smell of skunk and poke-grass wafted by. Crickets sawed their legs together like a Russian orchestra, and there wasn't a car in sight. I crossed the yellow line, back and forth in wide arcs. There was a bolt of heat lightning, way off over the trees, a *wha-CRACK* that gave me goose bumps. It wasn't going to rain, it was just the sky letting me know it was there. *Wha-CRACK!* I stood on the pedals, hands raised. The ground whirred and plants whirred and it was like being in on a secret, alone in the middle of it all. I downshifted, trying for a wheelie and getting about an eighth of an inch off the ground. *SWEET!*

A pair of headlights crested the hill. They were way behind, and then I barely had time to take a breath before they were *right* behind me. An engine growled, LOUD, then louder, the car roaring past, too fast and too close as I skidded to the side of the road.

"Nice driving, GENIUS!" I yelled, the car already gone, over the hill in a wisp of exhaust. Top-notch insult, Stan. Way to crush them, verbally and emotionally. "Genius" was what Keith usually called me (obviously without having read any of my scripts). It's a word that tends to lurk. My mother never says anything ("genius"), and my father never says anything ("genius"), but I know they sometimes look at me strangely, not because I'm strange (even though I am) but because I just said something that probably should have come out of someone else's mouth. Someone older and smarter and less Stan-like. Which is amazing, since when I was in second grade I could barely write at all. My classmates all made it to advanced cursive, penning capital *C*'s and ornate *T*'s and generally making the teachers happy with their evident potential. My handwriting was so bad they thought I might have a tumor. First I was sent to the doctor. No tumor. So then they thought I might be Just Plain Dumb.

Administrator: "Does he drool?"

Teacher: "I don't think so."

Administrator: "Does he eat glue?"

Teacher: "Not that I've seen."

Administrator: "Does he frequently sniff his fingertips?"

Teacher: "Actually, now that you mention it . . ."

Administrator: "Let's test him."

So they showed me circles and squares and triangles and asked which didn't belong (duh, the Stan one). Or read analogies, like "Fish is to water as Stan is to . . ." (drowned?). Afterward, I was sure they were right and I was even dumber than your run-of-the-mill finger-sniffer, but the results came back and after a lot of hemming and hawing and calls to the state testing board and calls to my parents and possibly even an aborted call to the local news station, it turned out I had an eye-cue of 165. Go figure.

I stood up on the pedals again, pumping away, working hard to make it to the top of the hill. Halfway there I noticed another pair of headlights. This time they weren't racing, just lingering on the horizon, keeping pace. They were round like the other car's. They were big like the other car's.

I pedaled faster.

So the teachers stopped caring about my handwriting or laughing out of turn or making fart sounds with my armpit, and pretty much left me alone. Actually, from that point on they seemed to fear me. My father said, "Most teachers top out in the eighty to one hundred range as far as intelligence quotient, and I think that's being generous, so naturally you're an anomaly." I was in second grade and knew what an anomaly was, so, of course, I went to my room and cried. Why would anyone fear me? I spent a majority of my time picking my nose or reading books about courageous Irish setters. It all seemed so *unfair*. At least for a couple of weeks, until I forgot all about it. I mean, how smart can you really be reading Dr. Seuss and playing kickball?

"Hey, guy, throw that here."

"Um, okay."

Faster

* * * *

The road flattened and I picked up speed, leaning over the handlebars and shifting into low. My tires hummed. The headlights kept their distance.

The real problems began in sixth grade, when I was taken out of regular classes and placed in Assisted Learning, which meant spending all day in a room with Ms. Cobble (cognitive specialist), Ms. Vanderlink (clinical child psychologist), and seven other kids bussed in from around the state. There were beanbag chairs and orange walls and an always-on coffeemaker we dropped crayons and lint and nickels into. Ms. Cobble was round, had a head like a squash, and smelled like *eau du* Velveeta. Ms. Vanderlink was thin and wore black turtlenecks and pointy glasses and seemed, to the exclusion of almost everything else, preoccupied with removing lint from her clothing. We spent entire afternoons playing with clay (making enormous-breasted sculptures of Cobble and then crushing them) and drawing (sketching enormous-breasted Vanderlink tied to a tree and shot with arrows.) For some reason, we never got into trouble. "Discipline" was apparently equated with "creativity stifling." No matter what horror we concocted, Cobble continued to guzzle her tar-and-floater coffee and Vanderlink continued to remove nonexistent fluff from her shoulders. It was accepted, after all, on some unspoken level, that none of us would ever be considered normal.

"Hey, aren't you the kid from the egghead class?"

"No. Aren't you the egg from the kidhead class?"

"That doesn't even make sense."

"That make even sense doesn't."

Punch.

"Ouch."

Still, every one of my classmates has gone on to great success. Millie Crown, her nose an endless faucet and shirt a bottomless repository, went to Juilliard to study violin. Paul Stark, extraordinarily thin and with a penchant for torturing Goober, the class gerbil, won a language scholarship and moved to Indonesia to live with natives (who later crowned him Sun King). Even Kate Bellner, who would burst into tears if you *even thought* about looking at her sideways, now writes a column on the "Young Adult Beat" for *The Washington Post*.

Have I mentioned my name's Stan and I work in a video store?

I approached a long downward slope, pedaling madly before the steep incline that led to my parents' house. The bike whirred as I leaned over it, momentum and gravity and wind, a sixty-second *mad rush* that made me open my mouth and howl. For one second I actually outran myself, the shadow-on shadow of peeled Stan-ness dragging behind the back wheel. But then, of course, the second was over. My shadow caught up and my legs surrendered to the rise, slowing, a sudden raincoat of sweat and gravity and inertia that felt like every minute of every day and almost everything else.

Also, the headlights got a little closer. I tried to keep my sandals from slipping off the grips.

* * * *

When the money finally ran out for the Assisted Learning pro-
gram (the Play-Doh costs alone must have been staggering) and
it was canceled by a unanimous vote of the school board, and
Cobble and Vanderlink were sent packing, probably to teach
poetry in a maximum security women's prison, and as a result,
for the first time in years, I was sent to *regular* classes, I got beat
up a lot.

Is that why, you may ask, *poor Mr. 165 eye-cue, you get
straight Ds?*

It's actually an excellent question. One Dr. Felder really
tries to "get at."

Dr. Felder: "How's school?"

Me: "Aside from every single second being just another
opportunity for embarrassment and humiliation?"

Dr. Felder: "Yes, aside from that."

Me: "It sucks."

Dr. Felder: "Okay. Then let's talk about how 'sucks' feels."

Me: "That's a joke, right?"

The truth is, I just don't know. At some point, in class, I
can't make my brain work. It freezes. Goes into sleep mode.
Winters in Palm Springs. The teacher will ask, "Who knows the
name of the estate Thomas Jefferson designed and built in
Virginia?"

I do. It's called Monticello.

But when I open my mouth, "Monticello" never comes
out. Nothing does. Or maybe something like "mayonnaise" or
"moray eel" might, which is even worse. Then everyone laughs.

Going Nowhere

They laugh, and I mentally attempt, like a dwarf star, to collapse in on myself due to my own incredible field of gravity.

I should probably mention, at this point, that I'm disabled.

I know, I know, it's totally not fair that I held that back for so long.

I guess I just didn't want your pity.

The truth of the matter is that I have a rare medical condition known as *Mentasis Futilis*. There's a telethon every year called the Mentathalon. You may have seen it. You may even have called in and pledged a nickel. All-girl lip-synch bands lip-synch, and fat comedians make fat jokes, and skinny comedians make skinny jokes, and out-of-work jugglers drop chain saws and bowling pins on their feet. Some guy in a sequined jacket begs you to call in and begs you to "pledge now" and begs you to feel sorry for me and all those like me.

It's a good thing there's 462 other channels on cable, because, to be honest, it's pretty unwatchable. Plus, there's no cure.

Okay, okay. I made all that up. I'm as fit as seventeen years of downing gallons of carrot pulp could possibly make me. To tell the truth, I actually wish I *did* have some kind of disease. At least then I'd have an excuse. I think the real reason my brain freezes is because I'm a chickenshit.

I hunched over, taking the long wide turn before my parents' street. The headlights were closer. A LOT closer. The car came up to my back wheel, high beams on. I waved it by, but it stayed there, inching forward. There was nowhere to pull off the street without wiping out in sharp rocks and gravel, and there was no way I could pedal faster. I looked back, almost blinded, circles and stars behind my eyes. What did they want? Was it Chad Chilton? Was it just some crazy old lady?

The car beeped and lurched ahead. The bumper almost touched my wheel. The engine growled and I could barely keep control. In one long careening sweep, I got to my parents' lawn and jumped the curb. My front tire caught on a log and I went over the handlebars, crashing into a patch of tall grass. The car laid rubber and sped away. I threw a rock at it, which missed by only about five hundred yards. Crickets boomed and my head boomed like it was hollow, one artery trying desperately to channel blood and fear and relief. It only took about a half hour for that to go away. In the meantime, no beautiful nurses came running up to wipe my forehead with a cold rag. I checked my arms and legs. Nothing broken. Mostly normal, if by normal you mean skinny and unmuscular. But someone was crazy. Maybe I was crazy. It occurred to me that I should have gotten the license plate. Sergeant Rick Steele would have gotten the license plate.

CHAPTER THREE
THE BLAIR *hippie Zen* WITCH *who sells spinach to strangers* PROJECT

I hid my bike in a furrow of gooseberries and snuck around the house, past the spinach patch and the tractor and the wood hut (Smith's Natural Foods and Gifts) where my mother's Zen-buddy Prarash sold organic (mealy) produce, and scrambled onto the back porch, breathing heavily. The gift hut cast one long angular shadow that folded into the trees. The whole farm was dark and crickety and scary, and it didn't help that our house looked like a haunted scrap pile, hunkered in the center of a half dozen vegetable patches, three wings of the house jutting like spokes, one still unfinished and the third completely unused. My father designed and built it himself. "Designed" might actually be the wrong word. More like "haphazarded." There were hallways that lead nowhere and doors that frequently opened to nothing, or even worse, concrete or brick. When I was younger, I was always stepping into unfinished rooms and smashing my face, and my nose was usually red.

"Hey, Rudolph, what's up with your nose?"

"That's funny. Really."

My father swore he had a plan, and was frequently sawing and hammering on weekends, but there were still staircases with no stairs. And rooms full of half-finished inventions. The Solar Fridge kept things warm. The Talking Showerhead didn't talk. When you said "Hot!" a cold drizzle came out. When you said "Off!" scalding water coated your back. The Talking Shaving Cream was mute, and the Talking Toilet Roll was always empty. So, really, "house" might be the wrong word as well. More like "maze." Or "trap." It wasn't until I was thirteen I stopped getting lost.

FIVE THINGS THE HOUSE I LIVE IN SORT OF
LOOKS LIKE:
1. A big pile of crap
2. Driftwood after a forty-foot wave
3. Where an extended family of orange-wig clowns practice their routines
4. The nest of Bob the Enormous Irradiated Gopher
5. The most embarrassing house in Pennsylvania

I disabled the "alarm," which meant taking a string off a nail; the string stretched at ankle-height across the doorstep and tied to a bunch of pots and pans. Strictly low-tech. No pin number needed. I felt my way along the wall and then crept up a staircase I was almost positive led to my sister's room, and hoped she was still awake.

Olivia lay in bed, the covers thrown off. She rolled over when I came in the door.

"Stanny?"

"Hi, Peanut," I said, sitting on the edge of the mattress and holding her hand. It was tiny and moist. She'd turned six two weeks ago. There were still birthday cards and banners and wrapping paper strewn about the room. I tended to call her dumb nicknames, like Peanut or Pumpkin or Big O. With anyone else it would be stupid, but with Olivia, it didn't matter if I was stupid.

"Where's Chopper?" she asked.

"Right here."

I put my foot on our ancient bulldog, rubbing his belly with my toes. He grunted with pleasure. And then farted. Social graces were not his strong suit. At this point, neither was running or chewing. He was half-blind and had two ridiculous snaggleteeth sticking out of his lower jaw, but Olivia was crazy about him. When I was little, he used to sleep next to my bed, but somewhere along the line he changed allegiances.

"Chop-chop," Olivia said, and then reached down and yanked his ear, which he accepted stoically. Olivia could do just about anything and it was okay with Chopper.

FIVE THINGS CHOPPER SMELLED LIKE:
1. Old hamburger breath
2. Old mozzarella

3. Old grandmother feet
4. Old turkey loaf
5. Brand-new sweaty dog-butt

"I'm glad *you're* here, too," Olivia whispered, sitting up and throwing her arms around my neck.

Okay, okay, I know what you're thinking: Stan's been reading *Catcher in the Rye*. Hey, it's not my fault there are two people in the world who are hopeless and also love their little sisters. Besides, that's a *book*. This is life. In fact, sitting there, I was again reminded that Olivia was the only thing, the only evidence, the only compelling argument I could make, just by her sheer existence, that the world wasn't, in reality, a massive and useless pile of crap. So Holden can go screw.

"Are we still going to feed the birds tomorrow?"

I'd promised to take her to the lake. Olivia liked to sit on the benches, where we'd tear hunks off an unsold loaf of my mother's organic seventeen-grain spelt bread, and watch with amazement as the birds actually ate it.

"We sure are."

"You promised," she said, ready for me to back out and disappoint her. No matter how hard I tried, it seemed like I did that a lot. Life kept getting in the way of being the person I was supposed to be.

"You're right," I agreed. "Now go to sleep."

"But I'm not tired."

"Yes, you are."

I laid her down and scratched her back while she

squirmed, then waited until her breathing became steady. As I tiptoed to the door, Chopper gave me a parting blast, a solid B-flat.

"Classy," I told him.

He raised an eyebrow and then rolled over and went back to sleep. I considered opening a window, but the percentages were against it. It might open sideways. It might open to a pile of bricks. It might open to an alternate universe where Chopper lay in bed in his jammies and Olivia was curled up on the floor with a ham bone in her paws.

I felt along the hallway, which narrowed and sloped downward, coming to a dead end, then retraced my steps, took a hard left, bent under a four-foot doorway, and found my room. I sat on the bed, trying to keep my balance. For some reason, it leaned to the left. The floor was level and the legs were all the same length. I'd measured them. Still, it leaned. It defied logic. My father defied logic. He'd also invented Bedsheets-on-a-Roll. There were a dozen sheets above the headboard, perforated like paper towels. Instead of washing your old sheets, you threw them away and just pulled out a new one. Was it environmentally friendly? Probably not. Maybe that's why I was stuck with the prototype.

I looked around the room and wondered what to do. There were the same books (either Nietzsche or *The Basketball Diaries*) on the shelf, the same records (either the Stones or Pavement) on the floor, the same posters (either Jean Harlow — *old school,* or Uma Thurman — *leather tracksuit*) on the wall, and the same smell of sweat-sock there always was.

Boring.

I could work on my script. *What script?*

I could work on my idea. *What idea?*

Anyway, I didn't feel like it.

I could go downstairs and talk to my father, except he was probably tinkering in his basement lab. Actually, there was no probably about it. He was definitely down there, inventing see-through earwax.

I could go downstairs and talk to my mother, except she and Prarash were burning incense and having "book study," which was supposed to mean discussing Buddhist texts, but really meant eating carob truffles and gossiping about people in town.

I wondered what Keith was up to, which was dumb, since it was a near mathematical certainty he was lying on a couch gobbling candy and watching some sport, which allowed him to lie in one place for ridiculously long periods of time. It also gave him a reason to yell, loudly and repeatedly, "GO! STOP! TACKLE! HIT!" without his neighbors calling the cops.

Then the phone rang, which hardly ever happened.

My mother yelled "Stan? Phone?" which also hardly ever happened.

I walked down(some)stairs, walked upstairs, took a hard right, ducked under a five-foot doorway, ended up near my father's "laboratory" (there it was), and then walked to the old plastic receiver in the kitchen. I could hear soldering or the cranking of nuts and bolts. With any luck, the old man was inventing an ATM.

"Hello?"

"Yo, Stan-dog."

It was Miles, my best friend. (Yes, I have friends. Sort of.)

"How many times have I told you not to call me 'Stan-dog,' Miles? Or, for that matter, attach the word 'dog' to anything, ever?"

"Ha-ha," he laughed, in his smooth and charming way. "Ha-ha."

Miles had a great name. Miles. Like Miles Davis or Miles Away from Home or I Can See for Miles. As a result, he was popular in a sort of goofy way that required no effort or forethought, and no one ever punched him. He wore the clothes he wanted to (odd colors and thrift-store — always clashing) and the hair he wanted to (long and curly and everywhere) and didn't feel obliged to copy any style. He was always invited to parties, and when he walked in, everyone said "Miles!" and even the blond soccer girls liked him, although he'd had the same girlfriend since second grade, Cari Calloway, and everyone knew, even then, that the two of them would grow up and be married and be smart and funny and wise adults and have a nice house with a library full of rare leather books and a pool shaped like a martini glass. They were also destined to produce any number of painless-labor, bright-eyed, smart and funny and wonderful children who would invariably go to eastern colleges and be on prestigious committees and serve selflessly as volunteers in African republics and wear comfy sweaters and come home regularly to help Dad rake the leaves.

You could see it all just by looking at him. Why in God's name he put up with me was still a mystery.

"Sorry, Dick Nixon," he apologized. "I keep forgetting you're DJ-phobic. Anyway, you wanna go to a party?"

Miles had the habit of constantly referring to me as someone else, usually some celebrity or historical figure, depending on the situation. He did it without thinking. All the girls thought it was cute. I thought it was annoying as hell. Also, I definitely, absolutely, completely did not want to go to a party.

"NO PARTIES!" my mother yelled from the living room. We had only one phone and she was hundreds of feet away. There was no possibility she could have overheard.

"How does she do that?" Miles laughed.

"Psychic hotline," I said. "She's really a Jamaican priestess."

"Anyway, Bob Marley," he said, "party?"

"I can't."

"Ellen's gonna be there."

My throat constricted. My brow furrowed. My cliché clichéd.

Her name was actually Eleanor, but everyone called her Ellen and there were many, many nights that I lay on the carpet in my room and said her name over and over and over again until it was one long yogic chant. I'd been crazy about her for a year, and she absolutely didn't notice or care. Plus, she was so beautiful it made my teeth hurt. Pale, with a small nose and small hands and small feet. She had a way of smiling, almost a smirk, that drove me crazy, one lip up and showing her teeth like *I know something you don't.* She wore sweaters with necklaces dangling outside of them and jeans with a tiny butt inside of them and she had slender, tapered fingers, like they were made for something more important than just fitting into gloves.

There was *one* other thing. No big deal, really. Just sort of a minor obstacle. A hiccup. Like your grandmother might smile after you broke her favorite candy dish and say, "It's okay, sweetie, life's full of little problems."

Ellen was Chad Chilton's girlfriend.

Or ex-girlfriend. Depended who you asked.

"Um . . . ," I said. "Ummm . . ."

Miles laughed. "You have absolutely *no* poker face, you know that, Johnny Chan? Absolutely none."

"You can tell over the phone?"

"Yes."

"Ummm . . . ," I said again. Ellen. Every single inch of me ached.

"Meet me at the bridge in fifteen minutes," Miles commanded. (He refused to come to my house on the off chance that he might run into my mother, or even worse, Prarash.)

"What are you afraid of?" I goaded.

"Man, is that Prarash dude there?"

(Was he ever *not* here?)

"Nope," I lied.

"You're lying, Benedict Starnald, I can practically smell him over the phone."

I laughed. "Okay, okay."

"Dude smells *funky*, you know it? And he's always smiling, too. His leg could be on fire and he'd be smiling away, telling you how blessed he was to be warm."

"Yeah," I sighed.

"I don't know how you stand it," Miles said ruefully.

"I guess since I have no choice, it's pretty easy."

"True," he admitted. "Now hurry up and pedal over, Lance Armstrong, and I'll pick your Casanova butt up."

"Wait!" I said. "Holy crap, Miles, I forgot to tell you how someone almost ran me over, and . . ."

I stopped explaining when I realized the line was dead. Besides, I needed time to pick out the right clothes. And the right deodorant. And the right face.

FIVE THINGS I PROBABLY SHOULDN'T WEAR:
1. An orange Speedo
2. A gold medallion that says "Love" on one side and "Hate" on the other
3. High heels
4. A chocolate mustache
5. One large Yogi Bear tie

Actually, the Yogi tie wasn't half-bad. But I settled for a sweatshirt instead.

CHAPTER FOUR
MR. AND MRS. *(no, seriously)* SMITH

Her name was Eleanor, but everyone called her Ellen, and her last name was Rigby, so she spent a lot of time explaining herself:

Typical Football Moron: "Eleanor Rigby? Your name is *Eleanor Rigby,* like the *Beatles song*?"

Ellen: (sigh) "Yup."

Typical Football Moron: "Cool. Just like the Beatles song."

Ellen: "Yup. Just like it."

Typical Football Moron: (loud and within earshot of all his pals) "So what's your mom's name, *Madonna*?" (Ha-ha-ha-ha. Ha-ha-ha-ha.)

Ellen: "Gosh, I never heard that one before."

So, we had a lot in common, given that my name was not only Stan, but also Smith, for the combined wonder of *Stan Smith.*

Typical Soccer Moron: "Your name is Stan Smith? *Stan Smith,* like the sneaker?"

Me: "Yup (sigh), like the sneaker."

Typical Soccer Moron: (loud and within earshot of all his pals) "So what's your mom's name, Air Jordan?" (Ha-ha-ha-ha. Ha-ha-ha-ha.)

Me: "Hilarious. Believe it or not, Cleft Chin, I've never heard that one before."

Typical Soccer Moron: (before punch) "What did you say?

Me: "Nothing." (then) "Ouch."

So, as you might imagine, we'd bonded over this likeness, during our one (1) wonderful, precious, life affirming conversation, the day she came into Happy Video with her father and they walked around while I stared, stared, stared, pretending to listen to Keith tell yet another (incredibly loud) story about either scoring the winning touchdown or preventing the other team from scoring the winning touchdown (his two variations on hero-dom). For some reason, just watching her, just talking about dumb and meaningless things, for the first time I felt like I'd connected with someone. Someone female. It wasn't like with girls at school, blond and giggling and beautiful across the room, sitting in the cool row of desks, which might as well have been in Moscow for all the chance I had. It wasn't like models or commercials or magazines or videos. For once it didn't feel plastic. There was something *there,* and I knew it was true because even Keith couldn't ruin it. Especially when he tried to show me off.

"Stan knows where every movie in the place is, don't you Stan?"

I shrugged, turning red.

"Watch!" Keith said, winking. *"Bull Durham."*

I closed my eyes for a second. "Third shelf. Far wall. Fourth from the end."

Mr. Rigby looked. It was there. "Wow," he said. Ellen stared at me.

"*Free Willy!*" Keith yelled.

There was a joke there, involving his belly, but I let it go. "Second cubicle on right." Ellen was looking at me like I was a bug. "Bottom shelf. Between *101 Dalmatians* and *Freaky Friday*."

Mr. Rigby checked again. "That's amazing!"

"I have a lot of free time on my hands," I admitted.

"Hey, Stan!" Keith called. "Movies with the word 'bridge' in them!"

I reeled them off in a low monotone. "*A Bridge Too Far. Bridge on the River Kwai. Across the Bridge. Graffiti Bridge. Girl on the Bridge. Bridges of Madison . . .*"

Keith was giddy. He stuffed an Almond Joy into his mouth and blurted, "Movies with 'pink' in the title!"

Ellen shook her head sadly, but somehow I couldn't not answer.

"*Pretty in Pink. Pinky. Pink Flamingos.* All sixty-eight Pink Panther films. *Pink Narcissus, Pink Cadillac —*"

"Purple!"

"*Purple Rain, Purple Rose of Cairo —*"

"Bill Murray!"

"*Ghostbusters, Ed Wood, Meatballs —*"

"Murray alphabetical!"

"*Caddyshack, Charlie's Angels, Coffee and Cigarettes . . .*"

"That's some noodle you've got there, son," Mr. Rigby said, poking his temple with one long index finger. "So, have you picked out a college yet?"

"Dad!" Ellen said.

"What?" her father asked, confused.

Ellen pulled him by the sleeve and they talked in low voices for a while behind the *Teen Comedy* section. I pulled myself by the sleeve and went in back and wiped my forehead with an adult video catalogue. In the end, Ellen rented *Casablanca* (what a fabulous and lovable choice) while her father (with his pipe and his sleeve patches and corduroys) chose *Bio-Dome* with Pauly Shore (typical, despicable).

"Hey, Mr. Movie Guy," Mr. Rigby called, "I have a question for you. Why didn't they ever make *Bio-Dome II*?"

"DAD!"

"Sorry about that," Ellen said, waiting at the counter to pay.

"What are you sorry for?"

So we talked about what we were embarrassed about.

"Umm . . . Keith?"

"Umm . . . my dad?"

And discussed our various names.

"Like the *sneaker*?"

"Like the *song*?"

And talked about our favorite actor.

"Duh? Bogart?"

"Duh, me too!"

And she smiled shyly from underneath her little black

bob haircut, with her pale, pale cheeks and delicate hands, and I actually added her total *incorrectly* (two times $2.99 . . . think . . . *Think!*), which Keith gave me crap about for weeks, and then I floated, absolutely *floated,* the entire rest of the shift just remembering the feel of her index finger as our hands touched, as I handed her the (incorrect) change and then she walked away, out of the store, out of my sight, away from me, forever.

Until tonight.

"Warm," I said, to the showerhead. Nothing happened. "On," I said again. Nothing happened. So I washed out of the sink and shaved out of the sink. (I didn't need to shave, since I had no facial hair, but managed to cut my chin anyway.) "Flush," I told the toilet, and it did, which was some kind of victory.

Treatment for the feature-length film titled
GOING NOWHERE FASTER©
Written by Stan "Sweet Memphis" Smith

Danny Green is a tough young kid from the wrong side of the
tracks who wants to escape his life of crime and violence
and make it as a musician. He's been playing banjo for years
and is really, really good at it. So good, it's only a matter
of time before he's discovered and offered a three-album
deal. The problem is his evil brother Denny, who is jealous
of Danny's talent and will do anything to sabotage his
leaving town. Including talking Danny into robbing a store,
Denny pretending he needs the money for his girlfriend's
operation. But then Denny peels away in the escape car and
leaves Danny holding the bag as dozens of police cars come
flying over the old wooden bridge that metaphorically leads
to the wrong side of town. Thinking quickly, Danny hides
inside his banjo case, and then escapes on the back of a
garbage truck, but is now on the run from both the cops and
his conscience, with only the hauntingly beautiful tones of
his banjo to lull him to sleep at night, and also the free
cable channels at the motel.

      Will Danny seek revenge on Denny? Will the cops find
him? Is his music career ruined? Does ...

      God, this is stupid. This is really stupid, right?

CHAPTER FIVE

SUNSET *is a bad time to be caught on the* BOULEVARD *of broken dreams*

I hid my bike under the rusty struts of the old bridge, which not a drop of water had trickled under since they'd built an Enormo-Mart three towns up. My mother (towering over the picket signs) led the "No Blood for Enormo!" petition drive, not to mention the protests and the blowing of whistles and yelling of slogans outside the construction site. Prarash sat in the path of the bulldozers in a yoga position and *absolutely, under any circumstances* refused to move, until the bulldozers got close and revved their engines, at which point he moved. None of it did any good. Enormoco still dammed the stream and all the fish died and all the frogs and newts died, but, on the plus side, once the inaugural Enormo doors opened, people for miles around were suddenly free to buy one-hundred-quart cans of corn niblets and pallet-sized lots of irregular diapers and jars of ketchup bigger than mailboxes. If you factored in the savings, it was probably worth it.

Miles was, of course, late. It was also pitch black. I was

suddenly positive Chad Chilton was going to come rushing out of the darkness and knee me in the spine, so I picked up a rock. It was heavy and sharp and hurt my palm. It was also stupid, so I put it back down.

Miles, like anyone named Miles invariably would be, was one of the few guys I knew who not only had his driver's license, but also a *car,* and not just any car, but a cool car; an old souped-up Toyota with no muffler that sounded like a Sherman tank and had carpet on the dashboard and incense sticks poking out of the air vents and a cooler full of beer in the trunk, which he sold for two bucks apiece, and he was always flush with cash and never asked you for gas money and was always willing to pay for Slim Jims and sodas, all the things I never had the cash for myself.

Where's all that Happy Video money? you might ask. Where's the huge Keith paycheck (which he tended to "forget," at least once a month, to cut for me)? Well, given the relative state of Smith's Natural Foods and Gifts, not to mention the fact that neither of my parents had ever had a real job, or at least one that would require they be *beholden to the Man,* all family money coming in, including a certain minimum-wage-video-clerk's minimum wage, was earmarked for family usage. Yes, I was expected to pull my weight. Especially since we barely had a car ourselves, at least one that worked. For ten years my father had been retrofitting an ancient diesel Mercedes to run on vegetable oil. Every once in a while he'd get it working and my mom would fold herself into the front seat and we'd all go out for a family trip, which was huge fun all around, except that we'd have to stop every twenty miles or so at a Burger King or KFC and then sit in the car while my father went in to ask the managers for their used french fry grease, and I would nearly die of embarrassment. Being embarrassed didn't seem to bother my mother too much.

FIVE THINGS LESS EMBARRASSING
THAN THE FRY MOBILE:
1. Naked at church
2. Solo contestant on *The Newlywed Game*
3. Caught in chat room for Hasselhoff enthusiasts
4. Fall down at Oscars, break Pacino's nose with flying head of statuette
5. Named Stan on purpose

"It doesn't matter what other people think, honey, you know that."

I didn't know that. It really *did* matter.

"We're all God's people, and she has a plan for every one of us."

"She?"

My mother would reach back her nine-foot arm and playfully rub my hair, which I'd long since learned was her signal for *I'm through explaining unless you're ready for an hour-long lecture.*

And what made it even worse, since we were already there, was that I wasn't allowed to eat any of the food.

"Hamburgers are poison," Mom would say happily, a paper sack in the trunk filled with the tofu pups and beet salad she had prepared for our picnic lunch. "You'll find that out when you study biology. In college."

College?

"Okay, what about cheeseburgers?"

"Those too, silly."

"If they're poison, then how come it's okay to use their oil?"

"That's different, Stanley."

"But how?"

"It just *is,*" she'd say, reaching back and ruffling my hair again, this time without even turning, with an arm that just kept coming. "Ask your father."

"I can't." I'd point to the plate glass window behind which my father would be shaking hands with a skinny man in an orange jumpsuit. "He's in *there.*"

"True," my mother would (oh so rarely) admit, and then my father would back the Mercedes (faded yellow with gray primer spots) up to the kitchen door, and all the cooks and dish-washers would laugh and shake their heads and watch with amazement as we siphoned off the rancid dregs of their Fry-O-Lator, first into the gas tank, and then into a fifty-gallon drum welded to our roof, and then we'd drive away smelling like the world's largest onion ring.

"Mom! Everyone's staring!"

"Shush . . . they're just jealous."

"They're not *jealous,* they're *laughing*!" I'd wail, as car after car that actually used gas would roar past us (the Mercedes's top speed, when it was working at maximum crispy-chicken efficiency, was forty mph), their occupants holding their stomachs and pointing and howling with laughter.

A dribble of oil would begin to run down the window.

"Mom! We're *leaking*!"

"We are not. Have some beet salad."

I replayed that scenario, with some variations, for about an hour, until Miles finally roared up in his Toyota, spraying gravel all over my sneakers, and held open the door.

"You're late."

"Yeah, sorry, had to stock up on provisions."

"Uh-huh," I said, briefly hating him for making me relive the McHorror.

"So, are you gonna get in, Duckfoot, or what?"

I spit in the dirt and then got in. "Don't call me that."

"Sorry, Rumsfeld," he laughed, and then peeled away.

"Duckfoot" had been my nickname in seventh grade, ever since my mother had bought me a pair of Superman sneakers. They actually had ol' Clark Kent, arm outstretched, flying away from the laces in his stupid blue tights. Of course, I refused to wear them. In second grade, they would have been great. In seventh grade they were a guaranteed disaster.

"Mom, I'm *way* too old for these."

"Nonsense. They're fine."

She'd gotten them on sale somewhere. It was time for stronger tactics.

"But isn't Superman just a pawn of the corporate power elite?"

"That's an excellent question, Stan, but, the answer is no."

"Yes he is!" I said. "He's a polluter! There's huge chunks of kryptonite all over the place! It's ruining the water supply!"

"Now, Stan . . ."

"I am not, no way, no how, *ever* wearing them."

"That's okay," she said, from way up in the clouds, her voice booming, "you can go barefoot. I did when I was your age."

"But . . . ," I said (how do you compete with that?), "but . . ."

Somehow my father intervened, and a compromise was struck. I would still have to wear the sneakers, but my mother would dye them blue. So she tossed them into a saucepan with some RIT dye and a few days later gave them back to me. They were even worse. You could still see Superman, except now he was a sickly green and looked like a flying corpse. Also, every time I wore the sneakers, my socks would turn blue. Then my ankles would turn blue. I looked diseased from the shins down.

FIVE PREFERABLE PIECES OF FOOTWEAR:
1. Nike "Air Broken Glass" high-tops
2. Crown of Thorns sole-wrap
3. Barefoot in Cow Field inter-toe squish
4. Oliver Twist brand dirty/wet rag bundle
5. Scorch Puppies briquette-lined loafers

Going Nowhere

"Perfect! They look great! Now, that wasn't so bad after all, was it?"

After the second day of school, when I'd absorbed an astonishing amount of ridicule ("Hey look! Egghead's got Superfag on his sneakers!"), I started to hide my father's work boots in my backpack and then change in homeroom. Of course, the boots were about five sizes too large, but they were still an improvement and sometimes even went unnoticed, despite the shuffling limp I used to compensate for five extra inches of toe. The real problem came in gym class. With shorts on, the boots were absurdly large, and I was immediately, and for the rest of the year, dubbed "Duckfoot." I was also punched before and after kickball (Hey, those boots are *cheating*!), until Miles intervened, just walked up with his hands in his pockets and said something like:

"Hey, are you sure you guys don't want to, you know, just leave him alone?"

All casual, no hurry, just a suggestion really. Which, amazingly, they took. And that's how we met. We'd been best friends since.

"My ankles are still blue," I admitted.

Miles laughed, shifting gears. We roared past pines and oaks and overgrown shrubbery. Large houses with many-car garages were set off in the woods.

"They still smell, too. Just don't let Ellen too close."

"Ha-ha," I said. "Where's Cari?"

"Meeting us there."

"Where is *there,* exactly, anyway?"

"Adam Pratt's. His parents are skiing in, like, Aruba or something."

"Aruba is an island in the Caribbean," I said. "I doubt they're skiing."

"Okay, Good Will Hunting, so they're snorkeling." He reached into the backseat and then handed me a can. "Want a beer?"

Have I mentioned yet that I've never been drunk? Probably not. It's embarrassing. I mean, I've tried a couple of times, but I almost immediately start feeling queasy and then more or less give up. Miles keeps insisting I'm just not trying hard enough. I've had plenty of chances to prove him wrong, but for some reason, don't. Miles always had beer, and always offered, and I always said no.

"No."

He handed me one anyway. "C'mon, Culkin. A man's gotta get thirsty *some*time."

I put the can on the floor between my feet. Maybe I was scared of having too much and making a fool of myself. On the other hand, since I made a fool of myself all the time sober, there wasn't a ton of logic there. Also, beer smelled like Keith. Anything that smelled like Keith, especially if it wasn't actually Keith himself, I wanted at least a hundred yards away at all times.

"Whatever," Miles said.

"Miles, who's gonna be at this party?"

He reeled off the usual names, Amanda and Wendy and

Sarah and Todd with two *D*'s and Jed with one *D* and the five different Conners and the four different Liams and the three different Ians, but no Stan.

"Who else?"

Miles shrugged. "I dunno. You'll see in a minute."

"No . . . I mean . . . is Chad Chilton going to be there?"

"Oh, Lord," he said. "Will you give that a rest? Huh? Chad Chilton joined the marines or something. That guy is long gone."

"I know," I said. "Probably."

"There's no probably about it, Shaggy," Miles insisted. "You think that guy cares enough about you to hang around this town?"

"Not likely," I admitted, secretly thinking he just might. For one thing, he'd promised. For another, I was not the world's luckiest guy. If there were a two-person Lotto, I'd always come in second. *Oooh, just missed!* If a meteor fell, it would land on my bike. If you had to pull names out of a hat, I'd get *Stan.* "But lots of weird things have been happening."

"Oh, yeah? Like what?"

"I've been trying to tell you. Like tonight, for instance, someone tried to run me off the road on purpose."

"On purpose? On your bike?"

"Yes," I said, knowing I sounded like a moron. "I think it was him."

"For such a smart guy, you sure have a one-track mind," Miles said. "You think if Einstein was worried about Chad Chilton all the time he would have invented television?"

"Einstein didn't —"

"Or the toaster? Or the ozone layer, or whatever?"

"But . . ."

Miles turned on the stereo.

"Not Nirvana!" I said, just as Nirvana filled the car like a broken Weedwacker. They were his favorite band. His only band. It was all he ever played. It was okay at first, *years ago,* but now I couldn't stand it. Kurt sang in his sad rasp and delivered his sad lyrics buried under a thousand miles of sad distortion. Miles had driven all the way to Seattle, nonstop for three days, to attend Kurt's funeral with a hundred thousand other goatees-in-mourning. At least he did in his mind, since he was about five when it happened. Still, he insisted he was *there.* No one ever pressed him about it. In fact, the only thing he ever got mad about was when someone mentioned (I know, I know, why would they ever?) Courtney Love.

Miles began to sing "and I pro-mise, I don't have a gun, nooo, I don't —"

"You have a terrible voice," I interrupted.

"I have a *great* voice," he said.

I turned the volume off. "Don't you have any Sinatra?"

Miles laughed. The little car tore around the corners, faster than the high beams could catch up.

"Slow down," I said.

"Shmo shmown," he answered. The car glided beneath us. It was like he was impervious, and so, by extension, for once, was I.

"So how's the script coming, Kubrick?"

"It's coming," I said.

"What's it called again?"

"Going Nowhere Faster."

"Oh, yeah, right . . . what's it about again?"

"Robot ducks."

"Come again?"

"Killer ducks. Made of metal. With laser eyes. They attack in waves. Quack. Zzzt. Quack. Zzzt."

"Sounds like a winner," Miles said, and then made a *ring ring ring* sound before picking up a pretend telephone. "Hello? Yeah, he's right here." Miles held out the fake receiver. "It's Brad Pitt's agent. They're interested."

"Ha-ha," I said.

"Ha-ha," he said.

Eventually, we began to pass lines of cars parked on the side of the road in both directions.

"Is that Chad Chilton's?" I asked, eyeing a jacked-up Chevelle. There were muscle cars naturally grouped together, hunkered down like wolverines. They all looked like something Chad Chilton would drive or own or crash on purpose and then stand on the side of the road with his arms crossed laughing maniacally. I tried to spot the one that had run me off the road, but they all seemed the same.

Miles punched me in the shoulder, not too hard. "Relax already, okay?"

"Seriously, though," I said. "On the way home from work tonight? This car? It came flying down the road, and —"

Miles sighed loudly. "Can we be positive from this point forward? Party? Fun? Girls?"

I nodded. "Fine. I have but one life to give to my country."

"Ben Franklin, right?"

"Actually . . ."

"Good," he said, then handed me my discarded can, which had rolled around under the seat and was covered with dirt and grease and God knows what else. The party was in full swing. Even a block away you could hear the music, or at least the bass line, turned way past distortion, some kind of hip-hop cranked into an excruciating mush, a frequency that no doubt was sterilizing every frog and lizard within a two-mile radius.

Miles gave up looking for a spot and parked on the lawn, with a one-handed flourish, the car skidding to a stop. The house was set back in the woods, a brand-new mansion built for a brand-new millionaire, lit up like an enormous candle. People stood around in the front yard, yelling, slapping five, tackling each other. I stayed in my seat.

"C'mon, Jane Austen," Miles called, already halfway up the driveway. "Your destiny awaits."

CHAPTER SIX

THE *very* **LOST** *and very lonely, and also fairly nauseated* **WEEKEND**

I woke up the next morning, late. My head hurt. Olivia was crying and my mother was trying to quiet her. I remembered I'd promised to take her to the lake hours ago. Ass. Then I belched and smelled Keith. Hole.

FIVE THINGS I FELT LIKE:
> 1. A dirty waffle
> 2. A dirty slipper
> 3. Dog butt
> 4. Wet cardboard
> 5. Dry cardboard

I walked downstairs in just my shorts and drank half a carton of orange juice, standing in front of the solar refrigerator without noticing Prarash at the kitchen table.

"Stanley, my friend." He smiled, brownish Zen teeth hidden beneath scraggly growth. I jumped, looking at him unsteadily. He was wearing a purple muumuu. Or a tent for a tarot reader. Two books sat on the table, large bound volumes. One was called *When Your Inner You Is Nearly Perfect-ish.* The other was titled *Advanced Concepts in Humming.* "I didn't know you sang so well."

I rubbed my eyes. It made no sense. "I don't sing."

"Oh, really?" he said, sweeping crumbs into a pile on the table. Then he wet his thumb and pressed it into the crumbs. And then ate them. I gagged. Orange juice ran from the corners of my mouth, sticky and unpleasant.

"Moderation," Prarash advised, holding up two fingers in some sort of spiritual (Vulcan?) gesture. I nodded, just because it was easier. He was about to offer additional wisdom, but I turned and woozed outside, careful not to let the screen door slam.

My father was in the backyard, half-under an old Volkswagen bus, fixing the brakes or the transmission or possibly retrofitting it to run on chocolate pudding.

"Hey, Dad."

He stood up, wiping his hands on a rag, and peered at me through greasy specs. He was small and wiry, hair cut short, and wearing thick glasses. Still, he was imposing. Thick wrists and calves. A man who spent a lot of time building things. When he was standing next to my nineteen-foot mother, though, it was a different story.

"You weren't driving, were you?"

I gulped. "Huh?"

He scrunched up his nose, like a rabbit, and then rubbed

Going Nowhere

it with a screwdriver. "Last night. On the way home. When you decided to have whatever it was you had."

I sighed and sat on his workbench and picked up a wrench, slapping my thigh with it. Chopper waddled across the yard and laid his jowls on my bare foot, which was instantly wet with drool.

"Well?"

I didn't want to tell him. Anything. A number of lies popped into my head and a tiny Miles sat on my shoulder and made suggestions about which were best. I pictured myself, in Aruba, on a beach, rubbing 40 SPF oil on Ellen's feet. Then I pictured myself, three hundred pounds later, becoming Keith, and no one, for any reason, letting me touch their feet, ever.

"I'm sorry, Dad," I finally said, which was true. I said, "I don't know what happened," which was also true.

He tapped my chest with a spark plug. "You're almost eighteen, Stan. I am well aware that nothing your mother or I say is going to keep you from doing some things we'd rather you didn't. Still, you need to promise me no driving. . . ."

"But I don't even have my *license.*"

He nodded. "What I'm talking about, Stan, of which you are perfectly well aware, is getting into a *vehicle* as a *passenger* when others, in particular the *driver,* have been drinking."

"I wasn't," I lied, which caused my stomach to knot. I tried to stop, but couldn't. "Really. I was on my bike."

He wiped his hands on his shorts. There were tools and metal scraps, templates, and engine parts all over the lawn. He pursed his lips, like he always did when he was trying to decide something.

"Really," I said again, like a parrot. A liar parrot. I saw myself with green feathers and a huge hooked beak, bobbing on Bluebeard's shoulder.

Is this where the gold's buried, bird?
Yeah, caw, that's where it is, yeah.
Are you sure.
Really, caw. Really.

Then I envisioned an empty hole and an apple shoved in my beak and angry pirates standing around a spit on which a certain parrot roasted.

"Well, riding your bike inebriated is also very dumb," my father said, scratching his nose, which now had axle grease on it, "but I suppose you get a pass on that. *This* time."

"Mom won't forget it," I said.

"You let me handle your mother," he said, stroking his beard, a long graying flag that would have made Fidel Castro weep with jealousy. I still had not one chin hair. None. Zip. It didn't seem fair. Also, as far as I could tell, he had never, in any situation, *handled* my mother. No one had. At least not without a stepladder.

"Good luck," I said.

He frowned. There was a loud noise in the kitchen, something breaking, and then prolonged humming.

Going Nowhere

"Dad, why is Prarash always here, anyway? Can there be a new rule or something? Where he's not here so much? Or, really at all? Ever?"

"Your mother finds him . . . companionable."

The screen door slammed. Prarash waddled out, a big wet stain on his purple muumuu. It could have been egg.

"'Companionable'?" I whispered. "Is that a Zen word for 'He Who Smells'?"

My father pretended not to smile, but I saw it, a tight grin behind his beard.

"Well, off to work!" Prarash called, as he waddled across the yard. "It is work that makes us both more and less present."

When he was gone, my father looked at me. "I understand your little sister is not so happy."

"I know," I admitted, feeling truly horrible. "I screwed that up, too."

"Want to tell me what happened?"

I began to recollect some of the party. Images flashed, like an arty French film that no one ever rented, me seeing Ellen talking to some Soccer Moron. Me deciding *Screw it* and being taught how to "shotgun" a beer can by some football dude (poking a hole in the bottom with a pen, then holding your mouth over the hole and popping the top, causing the beer to rush down your throat all at once), and then giving everyone an *extremely dull* lecture on the actual physics that caused the shotgun process to work. I recalled being thrown into the pool, and then surfacing and seeing Ellen still talking to the Soccer Moron, looking down shyly and holding her hands behind her back and giggling. I remember having another shotgun but this time keeping the physics to myself, then telling Miles and Cari how much I loved them and how they were going to get married and have perfect children, and Cari telling me how sweet I was and Miles calling me "Oprah," and then Cari found me a towel and Miles was talking to Ellen, but I don't remember anything after that.

As if reading my mind, my father said, "You lay on the lawn and sang some Beatles song at the top of your lungs over and over until I came out and had to carry you in."

"Oh, God," I said.

"Nope, not much to do with God," he sighed. "My understanding is that it mostly has to do with a chemical reaction called fermentation."

"I'm sorry, Dad."

"Is it a girl?" he asked.

"Umm . . ."

"You don't need to answer," he said, holding up his hand. "It's *always* a girl."

I blushed. I slapped my leg with the wrench.

"Even so," he said, "that's no excuse. The point is, now you need to make a decision. Is that person, that *man,* lying on our front lawn like a tuneless otter, is that who you want to *be*?"

I nodded. I didn't deserve his reasonableness. I didn't deserve the understanding from this greasy, squinting man in ancient paint-spackled safari shorts, or from anyone else. I burned with embarrassment. Chopper looked up at me with rheumy eyes, a sympathetic expression that knew the score.

"Dad?"

"Yeah?"

"Why did you name him *Chopper*?"

He scratched his beard with a volt converter. "Well, I seem to recall your mother wanted to name him *Twinkle,* so I guess I thought just about anything else was okay with me."

"Yeah, sure," I said, "but was it his teeth?"

Chopper used to have three teeth, until we found one embedded in the leg of the sofa, and since then it's just been the pair. My mother makes him special beef-flavored tofu nuggets because even Alpo is too hard for him to chew.

"No, I think it was the expression of flatulence."

"Huh?" I said, too beer-addled to put it together.

"Cuts farts?" he said. "Get it? *Chopper*?"

I slapped my forehead like the fourth Stooge. "I can't believe you never told me that."

"Well," he said, "some things are worth waiting for."

He began to pour small cans of liquids into larger cans. He arranged his tools, most of them handmade.

"It's so weird, Dad," I said. "You actually have this, like, sense of humor all of a sudden."

He shrugged, coiling wire into a figure eight. "You want to hear something else funny? C'mon in for pancakes. I'm making 'em."

Chopper, receiving the word "pancake" on some mysterious dog frequency, rose from his coma and stood, loosing a rope of drool. Pancakes *were* funny. My father cooked like he invented. Toss some stuff in a bucket and see what happened.

"You going to use flour this time?"

"No chance." He laughed, wiping his palms in the grass. Chopper wobbled toward the house. As we followed, my father leaned over and whispered, "So what's she look like?"

CHAPTER SEVEN
LORD OF THE *very crunchy and salty and delicious* pRINGleS

I was half an hour late for my shift. Keith frowned as I walked into his office.

"You, Stan, smell like beer. Beers."

"You probably forgot to wash your upper lip," I told him. He didn't laugh.

"I don't feel very good," I admitted.

"Not smart, Stan," he said.

I nodded and began going through the returns. Eighty percent of them starred Arnold or Barbra or a Baldwin brother. Not a good sign.

THE FIVE BALDWIN BROTHERS:
1. Alec
2. Daniel
3. Stephen
4. Billy
5. Zeppo

FIVE GOOD MOVIES STARRING ANY GIVEN BALDWIN:
  1.
  2.
  3.
  4.
  5. *Glengarry Glen Ross*

When I had all the videos stacked, Keith came up to me. I tried to cut him off. "Keith, do you have *any idea* how much lecturing I've already absorbed today?"

He pulled up his pants. "As a matter of fact, I do. This morning your mother called. Since I didn't answer, she waited four minutes, and then called again. And again. And again."

"Oh," I said, slumping. "Sorry."

Keith was scared of my mother. It proved his brain was still working.

"See, Stan, the thing is, I don't get paid enough to get woken up by your mother, you know what I mean? It's just not in my *job description.* Closing up? Sure. Doing the books? Sure. Talking to your mother? No. Especially before I've had my Wheaties."

"Sorry."

"She's worried. It seems a certain desk clerk is not meeting expectations. Normally, I'd give her a 'So what?' and hang up like I would on anyone who calls before noon, but I like you, Stan. Why? Hell if I know. Still, I did you a favor and told her you were a good boy. I told her you work hard and have a bright future, which we both know is horseshit, so right there you owe me. I may have to deduct it from your check."

"Okay," I said.

"Personally, I don't care what you do. College? No college? Ho-hum. Doctor, lawyer, thief? *Whatever.*"

He took a deep breath, eyeballing the candy display, before deciding against it. "As you know, Stan, from the many long and entertaining stories I've told you, hanging out in Millville with the kegs and the cars and the partying is *my* territory, right? Mine. Not yours. *Capiche?*"

He actually said *"capiche."* It was like Sonny Corleone chewing out his counselor at Jenny Craig. Still, for the first time since I'd worked there, Keith was dead-on no-fooling serious. He pressed his bulk toward me. It was frightening and I didn't answer.

"I asked you a question."

I knew exactly what he was saying. He was trading a week's worth of stories about touchdowns for one second of acknowledgment that he was The Boss, and therefore, had a valid point.

"Keith . . . ," I began, and then stopped. My head hurt and I needed about six gallons of water. "You're right. Okay?"

He nodded, almost satisfied, like his burger was gone but at least he still had some fries left. "So is it that Carl Turd guy?" he asked. "Is *that* what this is all about?"

"Chad Chilton," I corrected.

"Yeah, him. Right."

A month ago I'd told Keith about The Promise, just to

warn him that it was possible I might miss a few shifts by the end of the summer, being in the hospital or in traction or a casket and all.

"Chad Chilton?" he said, scratching his chin. "I think I played football with his brother."

"You probably played with his sister."

He ignored me. "What's he look like?"

So I explained how Chad Chilton had started shaving in second grade. How he had a hairy chest and a fast car and wore sunglasses and didn't look stupid in them. How his father was in jail and he had a reserved cafeteria table and a reserved parking spot and the teachers never called on him in class or scolded him about a lack of homework. How he pushed his bangs back from his forehead as an answer to most questions and almost always had an unlit Marlboro in the corner of his mouth.

"Wow," Keith finally said. "Sounds like you're screwed."

"Thanks a lot."

"No problemo," he said, and then went back to leafing through adult video catalogues. By the end of the day I was almost ready, for the very first time, to be disappointed in Keith. But after we closed, he took me in back and tried to give me some boxing lessons. He huffed and jabbed and parried and hooked in little circles, surprisingly light on his feet. I learned absolutely nothing, but it was fun and we only stopped after he got carried away and punched an enormous hole in the plaster above his desk.

"Whatever. All I'm saying, Multiplication Stan, is that Party Stan isn't your style."

"I *have* no style," I said. "I think that's the problem. Plus, someone tried to run me over last night."

"So it's a girl," he pronounced.

"God!" I said, exasperated. "NO, you meathead, it IS NOT a girl."

"Meathead?"

He raised an eyebrow and then admired his reflection in a plastic video case, which was physically impossible. He smiled. You couldn't insult Keith. He had way too much padding.

"It's *always* a girl," he declared.

I threw my arms up, exasperated, which was a mistake, since I'd been holding a stack of videos. They clattered to the floor. Keith stepped around them gingerly. "I may have to charge you for that."

"Fine. Also, someone tried to run me over last night."

"Listen," he said, "I'm heading over to Cloony's for some research. Don't forget to do the books."

"I won't. Someone tried to run me over last night."

"Good. Also? Stan?"

"Yeah?"

"If your mother calls me at the bar, you're fired."

A half hour before closing, Keith was still gone, and I'd rented out one video, come up with zero script ideas, and answered four questions about college ("No clue, sorry").

Then some guy came in and tried to rent a Hugh Grant movie.

"You don't want that," I said. I handed him a copy of *Key Largo.* "Here, try this."

"Um . . . ," the guy said, confused. "Um, no . . . this is what my wife asked for."

"Trust me," I said, only half smiling. He only half smiled back. We both stared at the box. In the end, he left with nothing, but I felt like I'd made my point: Hugh Grant should be illegal.

Another guy walked up to the register. He wore a nice pinstripe suit.

"Do you sell cameras?"

I looked around the store, which was composed entirely of cheap wire shelving that held videos and DVDs. No cameras. Anywhere. No pictures of cameras or boxes of cameras or camera price lists. I looked behind me, and then at the ceiling. I lifted a piece of paper and peered under it.

"Sorry."

He sighed, and then loosened his tie, dejected.

"But," I said, "we *do* have a copy of *Peeping Tom.* I know it's not a camera, but it's a movie about a guy who *kills* people with a camera."

The guy looked up, excited. "Really?"

I pointed out the box. He rented it. Another satisfied customer. As Pinstripe stepped out the door, Ellen Rigby walked in.

Not only *in,* she actually came up to the counter. I closed my hand in the rewind machine, just to make sure I wasn't hallucinating. It didn't hurt a bit.

Going Nowhere

"You seemed like you were having a good time last night."

I flushed. Almost exactly the color of the sign that read LATE FEE above my head. "I'm not so good at parties," I admitted, accidentally leaning against the register, which caused the error alarm to go off, high-pitched and annoying. I slapped at the buttons until it stopped.

"Me neither," she said.

I frowned. "You seemed to be doing okay. With the soccer guy and all."

She laughed. "Conner? *Puh-lease.*"

"How do you tell them apart?" I asked. "All the Conners and Liams and Ians?"

"They have tags," she said, deadpan, "behind their ears. Like bald eagles."

"Tags," I said. "Ha."

We looked at each other. The store was empty. She was wearing a pink top and white pants that showed her (beautiful) ankles. Her hair was held back with a barrette and she wore tiny round glasses. I realized my mouth was open, so I decided to say something. Anything.

"I'm working on a script."

"Really?" she said, raising an eyebrow. "What's it about?"

"It's a love story," I said, like an utter moron.

She laughed, and then pointed to the *Adult* section, which was actually just a converted closet with a green curtain hanging in front. "What's in there?"

"Ummm . . . ," I said. "It's umm . . ."

"It's okay. I was kidding. You don't have to explain."

"Oh," I said. "Okay, yeah. I get it."

"Anyway, the reason I'm here? I need a movie. I thought maybe you could give me a suggestion."

My chest swelled. Home run. If there was one thing in the world that I could *definitely* do, it was suggest a movie. Of course, then my mind went completely blank. *Mentasis Futilis.*

"Um, sure," I stalled. "What kind?"

"Oh, just about anything. Except no guns, explosions, effects, aliens, time traveling, hockey masks, or Pauly Shore."

"Tough," I laughed, relieved. The clouds parted. The telethon kicked in. "A very hard request."

"If you're not up to it, I can try somewhere else."

I shook my head. "There is nowhere else."

"True," she admitted.

"Besides, I know the perfect movie."

"Really? What?"

FOUR POSSIBLE MOVIES TO SUGGEST FOR ELLEN:
1. *Endless Love III: StanEllen's Paradise*
2. William Shakespeare's *Staneo and Ellenette*
3. *Bill and Ted and Stan and Ellen's Big Adventure*
4. *Stantanic* — Director's Cut

"*One Flew Over the Cuckoo's Nest,*" I finally said. "It's an early Jack Nicholson. One of my favorites."

I went and got the box and handed it to her. "It's smart and funny and no one wears a rubber head."

"I'll take it," she said, without even looking, the ultimate gesture of trust.

"Are you *sure*?"

"If you are."

Right there, at that very second, I resolved to be a better person.

But first, I rang her up.

Ellen gave me the money and I gave her back the (correct) change, and then when I was bagging her video I realized I should have just *given* her the movie for free, so I got flustered and blurted out, without thinking, no "Monticello," or "mayonnaise," for once, not only the right word coming from my mouth, but a whole sentence:

"I'm taking my little sister to the lake on Sunday to feed the ducks. You wanna come?"

Treatment for the feature-length film titled
GOING NOWHERE FASTER©
Written by Stan "Night Train" Smith

This movie is about a boy named Ted. And his love for a fish.
The fish's name is Bertrand Russell. Bertrand Russell is a
mackerel with big fins and a spotted tail. This is a movie
with plenty of heart and a touch of magic. This is a movie
told with such sensitivity and melancholy that the reader
may well suspect the author (Me. Stan.) to be experiencing
menopause. Bertrand Russell is kept in the family bathtub,
which Ted's older sisters insist promotes substandard
hygiene. There are many shots of Ted and his sisters, wet
nylons hanging over shower rods, the girls giggling and
sharing clothes, their teasing of Ted, his retreats to the
bathroom to talk to Bertrand Russell. Yes, Ted will actually
speak aloud to the fish, which is a running joke at family
dinners. Through these monologues with Bertrand Russell, we
will come to understand Ted, his hopes and dreams. The
story's conflict will involve Ted's mother, who will succumb
to her inner rage by killing Bertrand Russell with a broom.
She will do this for some insignificant reason, a broken tea
cup or the buzz of a determined fly, but we will understand
her true anger comes from having been left by Ted's father,
who long ago skulked off in the middle of the night bound
for Norway and the subtle charms of the women of Oslo. The
mother, in the shocking last scene, cooks Bertrand Russell
and feeds him to her unwitting children. Ted will eat with
relish, only later discovering the empty tub. The final scene

Going Nowhere

is of Ted, now an adult, lying on the couch in his therapist's office, discussing his lifelong case of dyspepsia.

Actually, no, he won't. That's dumb. A boy talking to a fish? Who wants to see a movie about a boy talking to a fish?

CHAPTER EIGHT
THE GRAPES *and other unpleasant varietals* OF WRATH

On Saturday morning my mother woke me to say I was working the counter at Smith's Natural Foods.

"Prarash called. He's going to be late. I need you to cover."

It was five in the morning. Smith's Natural opened early so that the local market owners could buy their produce for the day, at least in theory, since local market owners inclined to stay in business never bought anything, more than once, from the store.

"No," I said. "I refuse."

"You've got twenty minutes to be elbow-deep in produce," she said, ducking her head and leaving the door open.

It was warm under my blanket. It was cold not under my blanket. I stared at the ceiling and considered my options.

1.

2.

3.

Going Nowhere

Nineteen minutes and forty seconds later, my arms were submerged in a galvanized bucket, washing yams.

"No. I *refuse*," I told my reflection.

"Sure you do, chickenshit," my reflection answered.

I sighed. Only six hundred more yams to go.

In the distance, I could see my mother in the lettuce patch, busily directing her team of gardeners, a trio of Guatemalan brothers, all of them named Roberto. Apparently their father was not only a huge fan of Roberto Duran but also suffered from attention deficit disorder. To ease the confusion, the brothers (with the creative weight of dad coursing through their veins) had adopted the nicknames Uno, Dos, and Tres. They were an odd sight, cutting at lettuce heads with sharp knives, while my mother towered over them, even with her legs in the furrows. She was a firm believer that there was *spirituality in hard work,* and no one got off easy. The Robertos referred to her as *"La Amazonia,"* at least when she was more than twice a safe listening distance away. I liked Uno, and Tres was okay, too, but Dos and I were friends. Sometimes on weekends I would hang out at the house they shared with their families, which my father had also built, parts jutting out for no reason and the whole thing leaning kind of sideways over the edge of our property. Roberto called it *"La Casa Loca,"* and thought the extra staircases were hilarious. I called it "The Dangerous and Inevitable Lawsuit," and thought the whole thing needed to be torn down. My father had promised to "straighten" the house, but was too busy inventing extra-long beds for my mother or cutting tracks into the ceiling so her head didn't hit the rafters. Anyway, Mrs. Dos would make a huge meal and Roberto and I would just sit in the sun laughing or kicking around a soccer ball with his kids. My Spanish was bad and his English was bad, but somehow it seemed like just by smiling and pointing I'd told him more about myself than I'd ever told anyone else.

"*Hola,* Stan!" Dos called, when he saw me in the shop. He walked over and handed me a crate of lettuces ready for washing.

"*Hola,* amigo."

"I hear you *muy* drunk *la otra noche!*" He laughed, holding his stomach. Dos was a big laugher. There may not have been a thing ever said, in the history of the world, that he didn't think was funny. Apparently my being drunk was pretty funny.

"*Dios mio!*" I said, hitting my forehead with my palm (which actually contained a yam, so it hurt). "How you know?"

"You is singing *muy bien*!" He laughed. "Also loud."

"Sorry," I said, blushing. There were maybe nine billion people in the world I hadn't apologized to yet.

"*Es* okay. I *gusto* Los Beatles!"

He picked up a shovel and launched into a quick impression of someone playing guitar, really more heavy metal than George Harrison, but still, you had to appreciate the effort.

"I'll bet."

"*Mi esposa?*" He grinned. "Maybe she no like so *mucho.*"

"Tell Mrs. Dos I'm sorry, too."

My mother looked over and saw us talking. She wore an orange jumpsuit and an enormous sun hat that made her look like a deck umbrella. Dos looked over, seeing my mother seeing us talking. My mother frowned, seeing Dos seeing her seeing us talking. He winked and then shrugged, picking the gap between his front teeth with the lettuce knife, and carried his empty crate back to the field.

I went back to my bucket. The water was freezing and my hands had turned formaldehyde blue. Only two hundred more to go.

"Okay, let's get crackin'," I told my reflection, and began flying through yams.

Amazingly quick.

Efficient.

Machine-like.

As the underdog at the World Yam Cleaning Finals, I'd gamely fought through the lower rounds. Despite a painful wrist injury and a lack of corporate sponsorship, I'd somehow, against all odds, continued to win. *STAN!* collectibles sold briskly at the concession booth. The crowd had, of course, adopted me as their favorite, *oohing* and *aahing* as I tore through the final pile, hypnotized by my sorting skills, the display of brazen tuber-handling. The clock was running out. A dropped yam would disqualify me, giving the championship to Chad Chilton, who smoked a cigarette, calmly working on his own pile. "GO, *STAN!*" the crowd chanted. Blond quintuplets, the co-presidents of my fan club, who coincidentally all looked like a bustier Uma Thurman and wore tight pink T-shirts that said STAN'S ARMY! (although it was hard to read because they were jumping up and down so much), cheered and danced in a choreographed routine, exhorting me to "GO FASTER!"

"Five . . . yams . . . left . . . ," I told myself. "Must . . . concentrate. . . ."

Four yams.

Three yams.

Chad Chilton looked, for a split second, nervous. He was falling behind.

Two yams. I could smell victory.

One yam. I could taste it.

Then I dropped my brush.

It fell in the dirt.

A horn sounded and I was immediately disqualified. Chad Chilton was led to the medal podium. He lit a Marlboro.

The crowd cheered him.

The crowd booed me.

The quintuplets went home weeping.

"That's more like it." My reflection grinned.

I'd been beaten in my own fantasy. My hands were freezing and raw. Prarash still had not shown up. I threw the last yam at a fence post, wishing it was Prarash's head, and missed. Then I stretched my back and started on the squash.

Was Fred a worse name than Stan?

Unlikely. There was no worse name than Stan. Still, Fred was bad enough to be in the running, which was a small consolation. Prarash's real name, after all, was Fred Buckle.

Years ago (at least as he [frequently] tells it), Fred quit

his job as a cell phone salesman in Manhattan, stormed out of his office, and handed his tie and Rolex to a cab driver. He gave away his other belongings, adopted his *true* name, grew his hair long, and thumbed out of the city. After a few weeks in his sleeping bag, under the stars ("Wondrous! Beautiful! Spiritual!"), he somehow ended up in Millville and was drawn, like a crystal magnet, to Smith's Natural Foods, immediately striking up a conversation with my mother. Undoubtedly the word "karma" was bandied more than once. Certainly, the concept of Zen was discussed.

Then my mother invited Prarash to lunch.

In the span of one serving of bulgur and carrots he managed to thoroughly annoy my father (nearly impossible), who left the table midspoonful and retreated to his basement lair. Olivia cried and refused (almost never) to drink her milk. Chopper loosened (not that unusual, but still) a truly damning gust. I sat, with my arms crossed, amazed. My mother, oblivious to the mounting evidence, offered to let Prarash sleep on the couch.

And he just never left.

He built a yurt in the woods behind the arugula patch, bought a lifetime's supply of white sheets and sandals, and within a year managed to convince himself he was Hindu. Or Tibetan. Or something. He also memorized many sayings and aphorisms, most of which sounded like he'd read them off a tub of margarine, but wasn't shy about sharing them, especially with displeased customers. His method of staving off the clamor for returns and refunds was amazingly effective. He would smile beatifically and tsk-tsk and tut-tut and reel off a few sayings,

"The force of Veda moves in one direction only, my friend," and before long, the customer would be too embarrassed or confused to continue.

Prarash worked full time at the counter, assuming, of course, as part of the definition of full time you overlooked the innumerable hours he missed because he was late. It was just that, occasionally (three mornings a week), he was a bit slow making it out of the yurt. Prarash-time had a life of its own. I suspected Fred Buckle-time wasn't all that precise either. I once suggested to my mother that ol' Fred may not have walked out of his cell phone job so much as been pushed out. She gave me a look that could have withered a brick. It was amazing the blind spot my mother had, a woman who could spot a less-than-perfectly-cleansed yam from a hundred yards but at the same time so readily accepted his excuses. Prarash got away with more than Chopper did, which was really saying something.

FIVE BETTER NAMES FOR PRARASH:
1. RumpleNeckSkin
2. The Mollusk
3. Curly Sue
4. Gonzo
5. Special Ed

Anyway, I stocked the chard and kale and mustard greens. I washed off the counter and counted in the register and worked out the bank deposit slips. (Picture Depression-era cartoon of Bugs Bunny opening his wallet and moths flying out.) I dusted the dried apple-head dolls and the incense sticks and the ginseng vials. There was only one customer, if you counted a lost couple in a convertible Saab stopping in to ask directions back to the highway. The woman felt guilty and bought one (1) zucchini, 62 cents of pure profit. I pointed the way for them, and then watched her drop the mushy vegetable out the window as they drove off the lot.

Prarash rolled in about noon.

"Stanley, my friend," he said, hands rustling under the sheet that was cinched around his belly with a friar-like length of rope. *"Namaste."*

He took his time getting to the counter, and then settled onto his vinyl stool by the register, letting out an enormous sigh of relief. I showed him what had been done (everything), and then what he needed to do (nothing but sit on his vinyl stool by the register), and got ready to leave.

"The ant is a fine worker," he intoned, "but it takes an enlightened bee to embrace the past."

"That makes no sense," I said, trying not to breathe his scent, which was more aligned with organic fertilizer than a neighborly swipe of Ivory.

He smiled generously at my inability to understand higher concepts. "Or perhaps, my friend, does it make *all sense*?"

His chubby fingers smoothed his sheet, after which he sniffed them, confident he'd made his point. We stared at each other.

"Fred, you have Twinkie crumbs in your beard. Are Twinkies enlightened?"

Prarash's smile didn't waver, but his eyes, following me to the door, were definitely a harder shade of gray.

Outside, Uno, Dos, and Tres saw me cutting across the rutabagas and began singing "Eleanor Rigby," badly, in Spanish. I gave them the thumbs-up. My mother said something and they went back to their lettuce. I had twenty minutes before my shift at Happy Video.

CHAPTER NINE
SPLENDOR *or something equally as unlikely* **IN THE** *crumb-strewn* **GRASS**

On Sunday morning I stood in the sun and scratched myself in a pair of uncomfortable pants. Why had I worn uncomfortable pants?

Dr. Felder would have said I was *mentally willing myself to fail.*

Miles would have said, *Stop scratching and think of something cool to say.*

My father would have said, *Why aren't you wearing the Teflon pants I invented?*

Chad Chilton would have said, *You think THAT hurt? Try THIS.*

"What's her name again?" Olivia asked, a pair of spelt loaves under each arm. She had on a frilly white dress and black Mary Janes.

"Eleanor. Ellen," I said nervously. The ducks milled around our feet, ignoring the bread. They also milled around Chopper, whose leash was tied to the bench post. Neither tooth posed much of a threat. After a while, a bird landed on Chopper's head, casually pecking around. He looked up at me, tired, long-suffering. I pictured him wearing a toga and an olive branch.

"Maybe she won't come," Olivia said.

"Entirely possible," I agreed.

Chopper woofed. Not a single bird moved. It was already hot at eight in the morning, the sun low and strong. It was also very late, as far as prime duck time was concerned. By nine they generally huddled in the center of the lake and more or less ignored people, bread-laden or otherwise.

"Stanny?"

"Can you call me Stan, hon? At least in front of Ellen?"

"Sorry," Olivia said. "I forget."

"Forgot. It's okay."

"What's okay?" Ellen asked, emerging from behind a pair of oaks, carrying a loaf of Wonder Bread.

"You're here," I said. A statement.

"She's here!" Olivia yelled, and then did a little jump.

"This is the Big O," I said, introducing Olivia.

"No, it's not! That's not my name!" she cried.

"Hi, Big O," Ellen said, and gave Olivia a big hug.

I wanted a big hug.

Chopper woofed softly. He did, too.

Olivia gave me the thumbs-up, over Ellen's shoulder.

"What a cute dog!" Ellen said.

Chopper was not cute. He was the mathematical opposite of cute. He was ugly. As sin. Or uglier. I began to question

Ellen's taste (quick analogous formula: If Chopper is to Cute as Stan is to Datable, then Stan = ____).

"C'mon, Ellen!" Olivia yelled, grabbing her by the hand and pulling her toward the water. Ellen looked back, allowing herself to be led, and gave me a smile. It was a smile that dispelled all doubt. It was a smile that caused car accidents and inspired sculptures and made grown men gnash their teeth. It should have been illegal. I was officially ruined.

So, we fed the ducks (Wonder Bread was a huge hit, spelt, on the other hand, was widely dismissed), and then walked around the lake. Ellen and Olivia played and Chopper and I just sort of stood and watched, trying to force ourselves to believe it was actually happening.

At noon, I bought us franks and sodas from a vendor ($11.14 with tax. I had $12.00 on me).

"These aren't tofu!" Olivia cried with delight, wolfing hers.

Ellen raised an eyebrow. I shrugged.

"I didn't know that was your parents' shop, the natural foods place?"

"Good," I said.

"They sell a lot of . . . umm . . . interesting stuff."

"You don't have to pretend," I said. "Believe me, I know just how interesting it is."

Ellen smiled and leaned against me, in a *Ha-ha we're all in this ludicrous parents thing together* sort of way. I leaned back in an *I'd donate my liver to science if you'd let me kiss you* sort of way.

"Mom's going to be mad," Olivia said. "I think I got mustard on my dress."

Her little face looked so tragic, a big splotch of yellow on her chest, I almost laughed, which would really have made her cry. But then Ellen went into action. She bought a soda water and poured it on the stain and wiped it with napkins and Chopper licked at it, and between them, they almost got it all off.

"Thanks. Thanks. *THANKS!*" Olivia said.

"You're welcome, welcome," Ellen answered.

Olivia ran down to the water in big happy relieved circles and Ellen and I sat on a bench, alone, finally.

Saysomethingsaysomethingsaysomething.

"So you went out with Chad Chilton, huh?"

Nononononononononononono!

Ellen laughed. She wiped her brow and wiped her lips and shook her head and coughed. "I cannot believe that's still going around."

"What?"

"That rumor . . . it's like the guy with a hook for a hand grabbing on to the couple's car when they're making out, you know? Some kind of legend?"

Makingout?Didshesaymakingout?

"So you didn't?"

"*That* guy?" Ellen laughed. "He's, like, older than my dad. . . . Wasn't he in eighth grade five years in a row?"

"Maybe," I said, trying on the idea that she was telling the truth. It fit pretty good.

ChadbadChadbadChadbadChad.

"Okay, he comes up to me in the hallway once, right? Not twice, once, and asks a question like *'Are we having potpie for lunch'* or *'Is this the way to detention?'* or something, and then all of a sudden I was dating him . . . all these people coming up to me, *'So you're going out with Chad Chilton, huh?'* . . . I'm like, *no,* but it didn't matter. The rumor started and that was that. It's actually pretty hilarious."

Yeah. Hilarious. *Hahahahahahahaha.*

Relief washed over me. And under me. It was like six Christmases, all at once. It was like an Easter morning where the bunny actually showed up with baskets and eggs and then we hung out in the backyard tossing a ball around or working on geometry proofs.

"Well, I bought it," I said, feeling stupid.

"You and everyone else."

"I think he wants to beat me up," I admitted. "Or run me over."

She laughed. "Chad? I doubt it. He's a pussycat."

"I thought you didn't know him."

She played with the buckle of her shoe. "Well, you can just tell."

"You can?"

We watched Olivia, down by the water, demonstrating proper crust-tossing form for a little boy whose bread arcs almost immediately improved.

"I've heard some things about you, too," Ellen said.

"Some things? Like what?"

Faster

"Hmm . . . lessee . . . ," she said, drawing it out, making me wait. "You're the sneaker kid, right? Duckfoot?"

The sneaker kid?

I nodded.

"You don't really have webbed feet, do you? Is that why we're at the lake? Do you live here?"

"Well, I . . ."

She laughed and grabbed my arm. "I'm kidding . . ."

"Oh, right," I said, blushing.

"And you're also the math kid."

The math kid?

What was the square root of "loser" again?

"And the chess kid."

"Oh, boy," I said. "Guilty on all counts."

"So what's five thousand one hundred and nineteen times sixty-two?"

I resisted the urge to show off.

For a second.

"Three hundred and seventeen thousand three hundred and seventy-eight."

"Wow," she said.

"Yeah, wow. Math."

She frowned. "Why put yourself down?"

I shrugged. Dr. Felder would have said my shrug was the product of an unconscious need for martyrdom. I would have said my shrug was the product on an unconscious need for a long period of Sunday afternoon Frenching.

"You shouldn't," she said. "It's actually pretty amazing."

"It is?"

"Of course," she laughed. "Don't you know how lucky you are?"

Lucky? I thought about Chad Chilton. I thought about my mother, and my name, and my failed entry into the collegiate application process. I thought about my webbed feet and how I'd choked in the finals of the Yam Bowl.

"Okay, but if you know about all the other stuff, why are you here with me?"

"What's so wrong with the other stuff?"

I didn't know. I held up my hands.

"So how's Miles?" she asked.

I was about to answer when Olivia ran up, holding some dandelions that had mostly fallen apart. "Ellen?" she said, all easy and straightforward and normal. "I like you."

I couldn't believe I hadn't thought of that. So simple. Just say it. See what happens.

"Thanks, Big O."

Ellen picked Olivia up and put her on her lap. They goofed around for a while. Chopper looked at me, annoyed, wondering why I didn't pick him up and do the same.

"Take one guess," I told him. He licked a snaggletooth and resumed sniffing my leg. I wanted to be with Ellen alone. More. I decided we could drop Olivia off and then go somewhere. Anywhere.

"Okay, ready?" I said, looking at my watch, which I

wasn't wearing, so really, I was just sitting there looking at my wrist. "Time for your nap, Olivia."

I was expecting her to protest, some feet kicking, maybe some crying. Instead, Olivia said, "Okay, Stanny" and, when Ellen turned, gave me a wink. It was too much. It made me want to put her in my back pocket and run away to Burma so we could live on the beach (with Ellen, too) just being smart and funny and understanding each other all the time.

But then, of course, the other shoe fell.

The yang to my yin.

The cross to my skull.

The chute to my ladder.

Because when we got to the parking lot, parked right in the center, was the Fry Mobile.

"Oh, no."

"What?" Ellen asked.

"Grrr . . . ," Chopper said.

"Mom!" Olivia cried, and ran and hugged my mother's leg as she stepped out the driver's side door. She was wearing tie-dyed overalls and her hair was up in some enormous work scarf. She wore big mud-spattered boots and knee pads and looked like some crazed escapee from a lumberjack camp. Of course, she immediately began inspecting the mustard stain on Olivia's dress. "You didn't have a *hot dog* hot dog, did you?"

"Let me handle this," I whispered.

Ellen nodded, unconvinced. I didn't blame her. My mother was a monument of organic righteousness. She was a pillar of vegan zeal. Also, as we got closer, the Fry Mobile hefted and wheezed and made all the odd inscrutable gurgles it always made. Chopper immediately began licking the bumper. There was no way I was going to let Ellen get in that car.

"Hi, Mrs. Smith," Ellen said brightly.

"What are you *doing* here, Mom?" I asked.

My mother gave Ellen a big smile. "Your mom called, hon. She was worried you'd forgotten your insulin."

Ellen blushed.

"Insulin?" Olivia said. "What's that?"

"Shhh," I said, picking her up and snapping her into the car seat.

"Ellen's a diabetic," my mother confirmed, to no one in particular. I looked at her with genuine awe. Not even five minutes and she'd already broken the sound barrier for obliviousness. I had the urge to give her a leather jacket and a medal and sign her up as a spokesman for Quaker State.

"It's okay," Ellen said, "but I didn't forget." She pulled from her little purse an even littler purse that held the medicine.

"Oh, good," my mother said, although there was clearly nothing good about it, or just about anything else on the face of the planet.

"I don't care if you're diabetic," I whispered, trying to make it better.

Ellen gave me an odd look. "Why *would* you?"

Oh, crap.

"I didn't mean —"

"Well, since I'm here *anyway*," my mother interrupted, "why don't I give you two a ride home?"

"NO!" I said, biting the tip of my tongue, which hurt. "We'll walk."

"Nonsense." My mother laughed, playing with her hoop earring, which was the size of a manhole cover. It was impossible to take a hint if you had no idea it was there.

"No, really," Ellen said. "I'm fine."

"Okay, who's first?" my mother said, clapping farm-calloused hands together.

"Mom . . . ," I began.

"C'mon! Up and in!" She giggled, waving us toward the door.

I swallowed hard. Her arms were long and striated and tan from working in the garden. In fact, she was one giant muscle from head to toe from not having eaten a *morsel* of anything that wasn't Certified Healthy for the last twenty-five years. She was in better shape than Jack LaLanne. She was in better shape than Arnold. My mother could grab Chad Chilton by the neck with one hand and make him weep like a baby.

"Okay. Sure," Ellen said, frightened.

"Great!" my mother said, as if the outcome were never in doubt. Chopper knew which side his fake-beef tofu was buttered, and scrabbled his fat butt into the backseat. I looked at Ellen, apologizing as much as the side to side movement of my pupils would allow. She shrugged, pushing Chopper as far as he would go, and then got in next to him.

Going Nowhere

As we pulled out of the parking lot, my mother turned off her book on tape (at least the twentieth biography of Che Guevara she'd read that I was aware of), and eyed us in the rearview. I was mentally preparing to deflect the *We took to the streets, We changed this country, We stopped Vietnam* reverie that seemed to be coming, but she shifted gears on me.

"So, what do they call it now, anyway?"

"What?"

"Like 'going out,' or whatever?"

The worst. An absolute disaster.

"God, Mom!" I said, longing for Vietnam after all.

She laughed and wound long graying hair around two fingers. "You know, Ellen, Stan never said anything about a girl-friend to me." She shook her head comically, gesturing toward Olivia. "Of course, he never says much of anything, at least not anymore. It was a different story when he was a boy." She paused, for a second, a one-woman Charge of the Light Brigade. "I'll have to show you some pictures sometime, Ellen! He was such a little cutie!"

I envisioned myself encased in a block of Lucite, like a paperweight. It was peaceful. And airless.

"Umm . . . sure . . . ," Ellen said.

"I know! You can come over for tacos!" my mother offered, as the Fry-O-Lator swerved in the road. "I make great tacos. How about Friday? What are you doing then?"

"Ummm . . . I'll have to . . ." Ellen said, stalling hard, but it didn't matter, because my mother was already onto another thought. I could see it in her eyes, unfocused in the rearview. What was coming? A story about me wetting the bed? *No, too obvious.* Me not shaving yet? *That had potential.* Seeing Dr. Felder? *Conceivably.*

"Oh! I know what I wanted to ask!" My mother reached back and patted Ellen's knee confidentially. "Do we need to talk about protection?"

The Atom Bomb.

The Apocalypse.

Ellen's eyes were wide open, a thousand-yard stare. She looked like someone had hit her in the stomach with a four iron.

"No? Ha-ha, okay. You know, when I was your age, we used to go parking, too. . . . It's funny that now you feed the ducks. Ha-ha, things change, huh? Of course, *my generation* had to grow up fast, not like you guys, everything free and easy."

Ellen turned away, looking out — or at least attempting to look out — the hot-wing spattered window. Even Olivia, half-asleep in the car seat, tried to deflect the nightmare. "Mom, can I have frogurt for dessert tonight?"

"Sure, honey." My mother pinched her cheek. "Oh! I know what I wanted to ask! Eleanor, were you involved in this *party* the other night? Your mother and I had a little talk about it, and I have to say, I really do not approve *at all.*"

Chopper punctuated her disapproval. Twice.

I held my breath. Ellen held her breath. We were at least ten streets from her house. The Fry Mobile seemed to creep even slower than usual.

"Umm . . . ," Ellen said. "Ummm . . ."

"Breathe through your mouth," I whispered.

My mother rambled on. "Well, I assume your behavior was better than *Stanley's.*"

Ellen looked at me quizzically. It was the final blow. The nadir. *Stanley?*

"I mean, he came home and started singing! Right there in the middle of the lawn!" My mother hummed a few off-key bars of "Eleanor Rigby." "*All the lonely la-la . . . where-do they la-la from? . . .*"

"Mom?"

"*. . . Father McKenzie . . . writing a sermon . . .*"

"Mom!"

"*. . . do they all belong? . . .*"

Chopper began to howl, joining in on the chorus. I groaned, squeezing my head between my hands as hard as I could.

It was not nearly hard enough.

FIVE PLACES I WOULD RATHER HAVE BEEN:
1. Torture volunteer in Turkish prison training film
2. Raw snail-gargling in France
3. On "The Dentists of Southeast Asia" month-long tour
4. Buried in a crate under forty feet of radioactive mud
5. Getting treaded by the Fry-O-Lator's front tire

Finally, like a miracle, or at least the end of a string of a thousand consecutive nonmiracles, the car bucked to a stop in front of Ellen's house. Greenish, she mumbled a quick "Nice to meet you" and then leapt out of the car, practically in a full sprint up the driveway.

"She seems nice," my mother said, as the Fry-O-Lator turned and lurched toward home.

I kicked the seat, hard. "Stop!"

"For God's sake, why?"

"I'm walking."

"You're *what*?"

"STOP THE CAR!"

"Stan, honey," my mother said, pulling over, "what's wrong?"

"WHAT'S WRONG?" I yelled, jumping out. "ARE YOU KIDDING ME?"

"Stop yelling," she said, "you're scaring Olivia."

"*I'M* SCARING OLIVIA?" I screamed. "*I* AM?"

Olivia did start crying. She held out her arms. It was all I could do not to pick her up and take her with me. My mother rolled up the streaked window, her eyes hurt and confused. It made it even worse. Then the Fry Mobile peeled, as much as the Fry Mobile was capable of peeling, away.

It took me an hour to walk into town. I went straight to the nearest pay phone, which was also the only pay phone, and dug out a quarter.

"Hello?"

Ellen's mother picked up. She sounded like she'd been storing the same two ice cubes in her mouth, with great success, since 1982.

"Hi, um . . . this is Stan. Can I speak to Ellen, please?"

"Hold on a moment, Stan."

I could hear whispering in the background. It got louder, and then something slammed.

"I'm sorry, Stan, but Eleanor is not at home."

"Oh," I said, and then kicked the pavement. My toe hurt. "Could I, um, leave a message?"

"That's probably not a good idea, Stan."

"Right," I said. "Then could I . . ."

Mrs. Rigby hung up.

I found another quarter.

"Miles?"

"Stan-dog!"

"Save it," I said. "Just come and get me."

"Umm . . . okay," he said.

"And bring some beer."

Treatment for the feature-length film titled
GOING NOWHERE FASTER©
Written by Stan "T-Bone" Smith

How about this for something you've never seen before: Vampires on the moon! See, there's a beautiful female vampire named Suzanna, who has recently been turned by her thousand-year-old master. Let's name the master something Victorian-sounding, Colin or Tristan. The master is seen in a vague but eerie montage, a glamorous Brit, a quick allusion to the passion of his bite, his ruby lips, his bloodless gums. But let's say, before we leave him, that our heroine has once seen Tristan in his resting state, where he's really a big lizard.

Suzanna, we will learn, from various blood-hunger flashbacks, misses her equally beautiful daughter, from whom she has been cruelly torn away. It is only the memory of her daughter that allows Suzanna to resist, yes resist, the urge to feed on humans. It's unbelievably painful, this denial, worse than heroin withdrawal, and we may spend a page or two with her in a cheap motel, sweating on a bed, roiling in agony.

It turns out the moon, though domed and airless, is a lot like any number of bad neighborhoods in Dallas. Suzanna, stopping at a seamy bar, sits next to a man, bearded, tough, world-weary. His name is Tom and he's a vampire hunter. After a few drinks he and Suzanna go out the back into the alley and begin to kiss. Just as Suzanna's will is stretched to the breaking point, just as we are sure she is

Going Nowhere

about to bite Tom, he pulls out an IV bag of blood, forcing
her to gulp the soothing liquid. Tom reveals, after she's had
her fill, that this is not in fact blood but a compound he's
developed. He calls it Hemo-synth. Or maybe Andro-platen. At
any rate, Tom is a scientist and he can save Suzanna with
this compound. She will never have to feed again. If she
comes with him, he knows where to get plenty more.

As they arrive at his vaguely churchy workshop, Tom
leads her into a candlelit room, revealing an industrial
freezer full of Hemo-synth. Her knees weaken. Just then the
lights are raised and she is grabbed by hooded men. The room
is filled with hooded figures who begin chanting a mantra.
Just before she swoons, she looks at him and says, "My
daughter."

We lapse into a long montage, where the unconscious
Suzanna battles with Tristan/Colin for her soul. There are
fiery abysses, a vacuuming of the mind, a series of unparal-
leled tortures, but in the end, her will defeats the master.
She wakes in a crisp, clean hospital room, to a smiling Tom.
She is cured. Her daughter runs in and jumps on the bed for
a touching embrace. Tom leaves quietly, asserting that he
has "More work to do." Suzanna and her daughter move into a
nicely appointed three bedroom moon-pod and go on with
their lives.

Or, wait. Does that make sense? And what happens to
Tom? Do we care about the daughter? And vampires are
stupid, anyway. Never mind.

CHAPTER TEN
THERE'S *not a thing* SOMETHING *absolutely nothing* ABOUT *Ellen* MARY

We sat at the mica mines, which was just a hole in the ground surrounded by rock outcroppings, and drank. I spit out most of the first one, but after that, it actually tasted okay.

"So she asked if you go parking?" Miles laughed. "And then *rubbers*? Wow. Harsh."

"It's not funny," I said. "You should have seen Ellen's face. She will never, *ever* talk to me again. Ever."

"Listen, Chicken Little, all is not lost."

"It's not?"

"Hell, no. Why don't I just talk to her?"

"My mother?"

"No, Kreskin, Ellen."

"How?"

"Whattaya mean, how? I'll dial her number. Some computer will connect the phone lines, it'll ring, she'll pick it up, and then I'll try to smooth things. Maybe get Cari in on it. They know each other, ya know. They were in orchestra together or something. Maybe the four of us could go out."

"Orchestra? Ellen plays an instrument?"

"You don't ask too many questions, do you, Alex Trebek?"

He was right. I felt stupid. There was so much I didn't know.

"From what I hear, she's going to Boston Conservatory or whatever. Music major. Saxophone. Already accepted."

"From what you *hear*?"

The mention of college, any college, made me wince. The mention of her leaving town made me wince. The mention of her being a saxophone player was almost too much. I took an enormous swallow of beer. I envisioned Ellen writing peppy little jazz numbers and then naming them things like *Round Stan-Night* or *Take the Stan Train* or *Mood Stan-ingo.* I pictured her blowing off college and us going on tour and me becoming her manager and booking sold-out shows in Munich and Barcelona and London. I pictured her sneaking over to my house at midnight and serenading under my window, playing beautiful and tragic little solos.

Then I envisioned Chopper howling.

I tried to stop it, but my fantasy wouldn't respond. I saw my parents waking up and then calling the police and my mother running outside in her tie-dyed bra with a baseball bat and Ellen dropping her horn and running for her life, and then I almost gagged, so I stopped envisioning.

"I mean," said Miles, "everyone isn't a loser like you and

me." He toasted, clinking his aluminum against mine. "Some people are actually leaving this crap town."

Miles wasn't going to college, either. But then, he'd always known he wasn't going to college. He already had a job lined up in Pittsburg working for a friend of his father's. A cool job in some kind of photo studio or something where they made ads for magazines and took pictures of models and guys in giant celery suits all day.

Which wasn't nearly as cool as working in a video store, but still.

FIVE COOLER JOBS THAN WORKING AT HAPPY VIDEO:
1. Freelance Nose Excavator
2. Tater Tot Press Operator
3. Quality Control: Paper Clips
4. Freckle Counter
5. Cool Whip Attendant

"You'd call her? Just like that?"

"Sure."

I lay back on the rock. The sun felt good on my shoulders. The trees formed a canopy above us and my arms looked almost tan.

"Or, we could just do The Plan."

Miles had, for years, been trying to talk me into The Plan, which was his completely un-thought-out and non-planned idea about taking a cross-country trip. Camping out and seeing the sights and experiencing the *freedom of the road.*

Going Nowhere

"Oh, brother," I said. "Not that again."

He gave me an annoyed look. "C'mon, Farmer John! We'll take my car and just hit it. Screw college, right? It'll be awesome. We'll be like Kerouac and the guy from Aerosmith."

"Like who?"

"The open highway, Stevie Wonder. The chance to *see* the country. Niagara Falls. Grand Canyon. Nevada Bunny Ranch. Don't tell me you don't want to check out California? What's the point of this whole script thing if you're not going to L.A. to drive convertibles and take lunches and call people on cell phones?"

"I know, but. . . ."

"Shit, Stan, the girls out there'll make Ellen look like your cousin Bob."

It was my turn to give him an annoyed look. "For one thing, I don't have a cousin Bob. Besides, how do you know? You've never been there."

"Posters? Album covers?" He shook his head in disbelief. "You ever heard of magazines?" He started to sing, like a wounded Beach Boy *"Well, East Coast girls are hip, I really dig the styles they wear-air-air—"*

"You have a terrible voice," I interrupted.

"I have a great voice," he said.

"Be serious for a minute," I said, getting annoyed. "So you'd rather have some girl in a magazine who's probably been airbrushed half to death than Cari?"

"Who's got Cari?" he asked. "I don't have Cari."

I sighed. "Miles, I am not driving to California."

"Fine!" he snapped, and then sulked. Neither of us said anything. He got up and walked to the edge of the rock and tossed pebbles down into the cavern. After a while he came back and sat down.

"I read somewhere they think this used to be a stop on the Underground Railroad," I said. I'd actually read it on the plaque at the bottom of the trail, where it said, beneath layers of graffiti, that they thought this used to be a stop on the Underground Railroad.

"Wow, no kidding?" Miles said. "Can I ask you something?"

"Go ahead."

"Who gives a shit?"

I sat up, surprised. He punched me on the arm.

"Relax, Harriet Tubman." He laughed. "Don't you know when someone's pulling your leg?"

"Apparently not."

He opened a beer and handed it to me. I shook my head. "I'm late for Dr. Felder's. Can you drop me off?"

"So you're late for Dr. Felder's," he said, his voice echoing in the caves below, which went *Feld . . . Feld . . . Feld.* "So what?"

"Can you drop me off?" I asked again.

"In a minute," he said, opening another beer.

Two hours later, I walked into Dr. Felder's office.

"You've been drinking," he said, as I flopped onto the couch.

"You've been charging sixty an hour," I answered.

Going Nowhere

"Normally I don't counsel patients under the influence."

"Normally you don't counsel normal patients," I answered, and then burped. "So what do you expect?"

He sighed, deeply, pulling at his collar. Dr. Felder was, of course, wearing the outfit of the Cool Young Therapist Who Could Relate to Teens. He had on immaculate white sneakers and ironed jeans and a tie that was a piano keyboard. He had a mussed but expensive haircut that mussed but expensive doctors on hospital shows seduced beautiful nurses with. He even looked like the kind of actor who played high school heartthrob roles, with a five o'clock shadow and a shadowy past, and after the series was canceled showed up on Hollywood Squares with a receding hairline.

"I will have to notate this, Stan."

"Notate away."

He also tended to use "lingo," mostly MTV rapper stuff, *Do you feel what I'm saying?* or *I hear you,* nodding like he knew what it meant or like if you went to his house and looked in his fifteen-CD-changer it wouldn't be filled with every Simon and Garfunkel album ever made.

"Shall we begin?"

See, *that* was the kind of thing that betrayed him. Using words like "shall." The Lonely Rebel, even after his series was canceled, NEVER used a word like "shall." It was what, in the poker world, they call a tell. In fact, despite his hip rep, it was immediately and entirely obvious that Dr. Felder knew less than nothing about the world, and without question got beat up a lot in school (hey, buddy, join the club). He only got away with it now because he had degrees on the wall and expensive sweaters and an office with a leather couch and a skull on his desk and a half-eaten tuna grinder on the windowsill, just like a set from a sitcom where the characters make jokes about Freud that no one but the writers understand.

Why, then, you might ask, had I not told him to stuff it a long time ago?

Well, for one thing, the school district told my parents it was either Felder or expulsion after I got caught lighting Chad Chilton's locker on fire.

Wow, huh?

I know, I know, I should have mentioned that before.

Definitely. Without question.

But it's like I said, I'm trying not to lie, and sometimes part of not lying is just not mentioning things, which isn't really a lie, it's an omission.

Okay, I know that's pretty weak.

I apologize.

On the other hand, deal with it, all this apologizing is starting to stifle my creativity.

Besides, technically, I didn't light the locker itself on fire. What I did was, I casually (okay, not so casually, in truth, *very* carefully) stuck a match through the vents, where it fell onto his leather jacket and his carton of cigarettes and his muscle shirts (Miles was keeping lookout), and then smoke sort of not so casually started to pour out the top. I have no idea what else we'd expected to happen. It's like, for a couple of weeks I joked about it, and Miles goaded me (you'll never do it), and then I joked about it and Miles goaded me (Ellen's his, not yours), and then suddenly it was actually happening and we were both too amazed to run. But the teachers weren't too amazed. The principal didn't fail to run. In fact, they ran straight for us. Mr. Camacho put the fire out with a quick shot of the extinguisher and then looked at me with disbelief.

I was nailed, red-handed.

In the end, I claimed Miles had just happened to be walking by, so he only got a talking to. I got a month off (suspended) and then probation (two years). I also signed a document promising regular attendance at Dr. Felder's Hipster Training Seminars, at least until the last day of school.

Which was funny, 'cause the last day of school was two months ago, and for some reason I was still coming.

"Had the urge to light anything on fire lately?" The Feld asked.

I sighed. The locker was the only thing I had ever lit on fire. It was the only thing I was ever going to light on fire. I'd explained this to him a million times.

"No."

It was also the only reason I didn't get arrested. No one could believe I'd actually done it (including me). It had to be a mistake. I'd never been in trouble before. Plus, Cobble and Vanderlink testified in my defense and much was made of my *eye-cue* and potential and all, not to mention all the wonderful

poems I'd written in Assisted Learning, and also how a perma-
nent mark on my record would surely ruin my chance to attend
the prestigious institute of learning I would undoubtedly be at-
tending, so in the end, I got off easy.

"Sent out any applications?"

"No."

"That's off the hook, Stan, and you know it."

I considered explaining to him what "off the hook"
actually meant, but decided it was funnier to let him keep saying it.

"I know, Doc."

"So how's your script coming?"

"Really, really, really great."

"What's it about, again?"

"An evil computer. With legs. That downloads people to
death."

Dr. Felder frowned. "What's it really about, Stan?"

I scratched behind my ear. I blushed. I started to explain
and then stopped. "It's stupid. It's full of clichés."

"Don't play yourself, Stan. I'm sure it's better than that."

"That's a nice thought, Doc, but the thing is, it's not. It's
definitely *not* better than that."

"Okay. So what's the problem?"

I pursed my lips and really thought about it for a minute.

"I dunno. It's weird. Like, I work in a video store, right?
I've watched a *million* movies. But no matter how many movies I
watch or plots I see, I can't seem to come up with a good, original

idea. I just keep copying the same things I hate, like I've been in-fected with Freddie Prinze Jr. disease. And then when I finally think I've come up with something good, as soon as I put it down on paper, it becomes just another dumb cliché. And it's driving me CRAZY."

"You're not crazy, Stan." Dr. Felder chuckled.

"What are you chuckling for? I didn't mean really crazy, Doc. God!"

Dr. Felder sniffed. He looked alarmed that I'd raised my voice.

"Maybe you just need some real life experience, huh? I'd imagine it's hard to be a writer when all you know is Millville. Hemingway traveled around the world and didn't even start writing until he was in his thirties."

I couldn't believe it. Dr. Felder had actually said some-thing that made sense. He'd given me some good advice. There was a real, genuine chance he was maybe, sort of, actually right. I was so stunned, I didn't say anything. So, of course, he jumped into the void and ruined it.

"How's it coming with the lists?"

I covered my face with my hands and sighed. "One? Bad. Two? Worse. Three? Horrible. Four? Beyond repair. Five? Really terrific."

Dr. Felder wiped his forehead with his sleeve. "So . . . any other concerns this week?"

"Umm . . . well," I said, pretending to think, ". . . Chad Chilton wants to kill me?"

"Yes, Stan, you may have mentioned that once before. Many, many times before."

"It doesn't make it any less true."

"It very well may make it less true, Stan."

"Okay, how about how someone tried to run me over the other night? And then there's the slashed tires. And . . ."

"Sounds like a movie plot," Dr. Felder said, chuckling. He wrote something on his pad. Then he rubbed mustard off his pants. Why didn't anyone believe me? It was the oldest cliché in the book. I felt like Snuffaluffagus's dumber little brother.

"Doc, when I'm dead, are you going to miss me?"

"No one's dying, Stan."

"There's a billion people in China," I said. "I bet some of them are."

"You realize, Stan, don't you, that you retreat into semantics as an avoidance mechanism every time you're asked a difficult question?"

"You know, you're right, Doc. It's off the hook, and I apologize."

"Good. Excellent." He beamed, notating some sort of breakthrough with manic scribbles. It was almost too easy.

"Am I your favorite patient, Doc?"

"You know I can't make those kinds of judgments, Stan."

"When can I read my file, Doc?"

"You know I can't let you see your file, Stan."

"Can I check out the skull on your desk?"

"Let's try to focus, okay?"

I sighed. There were at least another forty minutes left.

"So tell me about the sighing," he said.

By the time I walked home it was almost dark and my mouth felt like a tennis sock, but at least the beer had worn off. My father was sitting at the kitchen table, an envelope open in front of him. He was rubbing the skin beneath his glasses, which made his fingers look huge.

"Hey, Pop," I said, drinking water straight out of the tap.

"Where've you been, Stan?"

"Umm . . . Dr. Felder's?" I guessed.

He nodded, looking extremely tired. "What did you say to your mother earlier?"

"Why?" I asked, getting peanut butter (organic) from the refrigerator and spreading it on a (Smith-grown) carrot (limp).

"Well, for one thing, she came home this afternoon and locked herself in our room. If I didn't know better, I'd swear she's been crying."

"No way," I said. "Mom?"

"You're on some roll this week, Stan."

"Dad!" I protested, my voice rising in an annoying way, but I couldn't stop it. "If you had any idea the stuff she said. How she ruined everything. Ellen will probably never talk to me again."

"Ellen?" he asked, and then nodded. "Stan, I know your mother can be a handful, but . . ."

"Dad, she brought up *condoms*."

"Hoo boy," he said.

We sat there, looking at each other. He played with his beard. He wrote some numbers on a napkin. He sketched a circle and then added it into a formula.

"Want a carrot?" I asked, poking one at him. He waved it away and then held up an envelope. "Do you have any idea what this is?"

It looked official. "Mom's resignation as Mom? Effective immediately?"

"This, Stan, is your acceptance and offer of a full scholarship to the University of California at Berkeley."

"*What?*" I coughed, an orangey spray of carrot flecks covering most of the table. "It's a mistake. I didn't even apply there."

"I was confused a bit at first, myself," he said, wiping the table with his sleeve, which was already covered with grease and made the table even worse. "It seems your mother applied for you."

"GOD!" I said, not sure how mad I really was, too tired to pretend. "Isn't that, like, illegal? Isn't it *cheating*?"

"I don't know. It may very well be."

"I can't believe this," I said, shaking my head. "Is she going to take the classes for me, too?"

"Stan . . ."

"Forget it," I decided. "I'm not going."

He sighed. "Your mother went to Berkeley, you know."

That stopped me, like a quick left to the chin. Had I been told about Berkeley? Was that something I'd just forgotten?

Did she get in on an Extra Tall scholarship? I always assumed, I suppose, that she'd gone to some organic farm collective where they wrote papers on tree bark and danced nude in the rain a lot.

SIX THINGS MY FATHER COULD SAY THAT WOULD BE A BIGGER SURPRISE:
1. "Your mother is a man."
2. "Your mother is a carrot."
3. "Your mother is part giraffe."
4. "I come from a heavily bearded planet and flew here in a bio-diesel saucer."
5. "I want you to forget all this college nonsense and write a script instead."
6. "Ellen Rigby is waiting upstairs in the Voice Activated Hot Tub."

"She was a brilliant student," my father continued. "Of course, once she was pregnant with you, she had to drop out, so she only finished two years."

"Why didn't you ever tell me?"

"She's a bit ashamed to have left without graduating."

"I didn't know," I said, a bit ashamed myself. My father had worked nights, putting himself through community college. I'd assumed my mother had as well.

"It may be time, Stan, despite your cranial capacity, to accept the fact that there are many, many things you don't know."

I put down my carrot. It looked like a gnawed zebra bone. I was an angry lion in the Serengeti. I could lie in the sun or I could eat an antelope. I could pick a mate or climb on a rock or yowl at the moon. Choices.

"Like, for instance," he continued, "how remarkably similar you and your mother are."

I laughed. "Me? Like *Mom*?"

"When I first met her, she was almost exactly like you are now. Difficult. Arrogant. Infuriatingly certain about everything and nothing."

"Where did you meet her?" I asked. "Like, on the Internet? www.Hippie/InventorLove.com?"

"There was no Internet then, Stan. You know that. Well, technically, there was, but it was owned by the air force and was used as a primitive . . ." He shook his head, annoyed. "Stop trying to get me off track."

"Are we on a track?"

"Yes. The one where you realize it's time to stop acting so self-centered. There is a whole world around you, but that doesn't mean it *revolves* around you. In fact, it absolutely doesn't. In the scale of things? Ten billion people on the planet? You are a tiny Stanley-speck."

"Wow, Dad," I said. "Don't pull any punches."

"You have no idea," he said.

"Just part of raising a teenager, though, huh?"

He handed me the envelope and got up. "It's easy to pretend you don't care about anything, Stan. It's also cowardly."

"*Dad,*" I said, but had nothing to follow it up with.

Going Nowhere

He pulled at his beard and walked toward the stairs. He opened a door that turned out to be a closet, shut it angrily, and then found the right one.

I was alone in the kitchen. Just me and the envelope.

Berkeley.

Ridiculous.

CHAPTER ELEVEN
TAKE THE *what* MONEY AND *where? how?* RUN

In the morning, the phone rang. I ran downstairs and picked it up.

"We're on, Stan Musial. Tomorrow night."

"Who *is* this?"

"You. Me. Ellen and Cari. Out to dinner, then a movie."

"*Aunt Judy?* I thought the nurse took away your phone privileges."

"Ha-ha," Miles laughed. "Ha."

"You better not be screwing with me, Miles."

"It's no joke, Doubting Thomas. She's all set. Took some doing, but it's done. Can you handle it? *Can You Dig It?*"

"God, Miles, you rule."

"Yes, it's true," he laughed, and then said, "I do?"

"What time?"

"Seven thirty. I'll pick you up at Crappy Video."

"If Keith heard you say that, he'd put mustard on your leg and eat it," I warned.

"Yeah, yeah, just don't be late," he warned back, which coming from Miles was like telling the sun not to be yellow.

"You know, coming from you —" I began, but he hung up.

Treatment for the feature-length film titled

GOING NOWHERE FASTER©

Written by Stan "Right Cross" Smith

Who doesn't love a love story? Who doesn't story a love love? Anyway, this movie is about a man and a woman who meet online. The man is a shy office worker who's been hurt before and has trouble meeting women. The woman is a single mom with a smart and lovable daughter who is doing her best to set Mom up with a good guy. Mom tends to go out with losers, and we see a montage of them, the Dumb Football Guy, the Porsche-Driving Jerk, the Crazy Conspiracy Guy, and the Guy Who Hates Children. The man and woman are about to go on their first date, and the daughter is helping Mom dress while rehearsing funny things to say at dinner. The man is having a comical time getting ready. A button comes off his pants. The dog pees on his socks. He can't find his car keys. Will the man and the woman overcome these zany obstacles? Does it all depend on whether the Nice and Knowing Maître d' (played by Hector Elizondo, or someone just like him) puts them at the right table? Will they comically order the wrong wine? Or frog's legs? Will a coffee spill cause a rift that needs another five slapstick scenes to repair?

God, am I stupid.

* * * *

The next afternoon I took a long shower and dabbed on cologne. When I was getting dressed, a button popped off my shirt. Chopper farted near my sweater and I tried spraying it with Lysol, but it smelled even worse, so I had to pick a different one. Olivia stood in the doorway and coached me on my choice of footwear. Sneakers or sneakers?

"The white ones."

"Are you sure?" I asked, holding up my trusty blue Keds.

"Definitely white," Olivia said, moving to the edge of the bed, her toes dangling in Chopper's fur. She squeezed and kneaded his ribs. He occasionally winced, but otherwise just lay there.

"How about this shirt?" I asked. It was a black button-up. Black seemed right, from Johnny Cash to Mötley Crüe, I couldn't go wrong.

"Definitely not black," she said, really giving Chopper the works. "Makes you look like a funeral guy."

"Mortician," I said.

"Who?"

"Never mind."

I put on a red shirt and then picked out my favorite jeans.

"Too wrinkly," Olivia said, scrunching up her nose.

I opened the closet and rooted around in a pile of Belt Turbines and Tie Engines and Perma-knot Knot Machines and Talking Shoehorns, and finally found the Smith's Instant Iron-a-rama. It looked a lot like a waffle press, but bigger.

"Are you sure you don't just want an iron? I bet Mom has an iron."

"Mom has never ironed anything in her life," I said, and stuck my jeans into the contraption. There was a large yellow switch on the side. I flipped it and nothing happened.

"It's not on," Olivia said, pointing to the cord.

I plugged the Iron-a-rama in. It made a loud wrenching sound before a huge billow of steam rushed out, almost scalding off my eyebrows. Chopper barked. Olivia yelped. A buzzer went off and I pulled out the jeans, which were at least twice as wrinkled as before.

"Try again," Olivia suggested.

When the buzzer went off the second time, my jeans were four times as wrinkled as before, and had a long black stain on the back. Olivia shrugged.

"Want to see what eight times as wrinkled looks like?" I asked, almost positive I had an extra pair of khakis somewhere at the bottom of the closet.

My mother was downstairs in the kitchen with Prarash. They were eating noodles out of the same huge bowl, a handmade ceramic one that had monkeys linking arms all the way around. I'd always liked that bowl. Not anymore.

"Stan!" my mother said. I could see in her eyes she was still upset about the park and the yelling and the Fry Mobile. So what? I was still upset, too. She was about to say something, then thought better of it.

"The young bee wears a jacket," Prarash said, slurping up a final long noodle, and then wiping soy sauce from his beard. "A yellow jacket. Ha-ha."

My jacket was black. "My jacket is black," I said.

Prarash looked at my mother indulgently. "Humor and the young, yes? But they will learn."

It was so annoying I wanted to scream. Instead, I said, "Mom, can you cash my Happy Video check? I don't have any money."

"Only if you tell me where you're going," she said, then started rooting through her bag. "Why so dressed up?"

"Umm . . . ," I said, aware of Prarash staring at me, and trying to ignore him. "Just a thing. For school."

My mother nodded, pulling handfuls of junk from her enormous pocketbook. Scarves and a brush and hemp tissues and a change purse and homemade beeswax lip balm and a scissors and pens and pencils and a pear and bracelets and a book (about Che Guevara) and a melted string cheese and another book (about Vietnam) and a can of dolphin-safe tuna and a barrette and a tire-pressure gauge, but no wallet.

"I can't find my wallet," she said.

"Didn't school end two months ago?" Prarash asked.

"Um . . . yeah," I said. "Summer school."

"You're not in summer school," my mother said.

"Listen," I said, resisting the urge to stamp my foot like Olivia, "I'm going to be late. Can you please just lend me some money?"

My mother looked at Prarash. "Is there any cash in the register at the store?"

He shook his head. "Not much. In fact, less than I thought."

"What do you mean?" she asked.

"Well, I don't want to say anything. Implicate any-one. But . . ."

"But what?"

Prarash sniffed his fingers. "There seemed to be a bit of money missing at the end of the day."

"That's impossible," my mother said, reclasping her over-alls. "You and Roberto were the only ones in the store all day. We didn't have a single customer."

"Exactly," Prarash said, sniffing again. The double-sniff. A bad sign. My mother stared at him.

"It is not for a humble believer such as I to cast asper-sions. Merely to sit and absorb as the world unfolds."

"Stan!" my mother called, as I slammed the door. And even though it closed, with a satisfying clunk, I could still hear Prarash chuckle and say, "Teenagers."

I was an hour early. Keith was behind the counter, halfway through a box of Twizzlers.

"Whoa!" he said. "Check out *GQ*."

I had on a shirt with buttons. And cuffs. And a collar.

"I've got a date," I said.

"You better." He laughed.

"How's business?"

He raised an eyebrow and scowled, pointing a Twizzler at me, which bent in the center and then was actually pointing at the *Horror* section.

"You didn't actually just ask me *how business was,* did you?"

"Umm . . ."

"Stan, Stan, *Stan* . . . you've gotta get your chops together. Are you going to say *ludicrously dull* things like that on this date of yours?"

"I hadn't planned on it."

Keith swiveled in his chair and came around the counter. He adjusted my collar, fluffed my hair, and then made me stand with my hips pointed out.

"That's better. Now repeat after me: I am confident."

"I am confident."

"I am in control."

"I am in control".

"I am one bad mutha."

"I don't want to say that."

"Fine," he said, going back to his chair and opening a ZAGNUT, "if that's the way you want to play it. But just remember that your old buddy Keith was giving stud lessons before your father was born."

"Keith, you're thirty-five," I said. "That means you were giving lessons to other zygotes."

"My point exactly," he said, licking toasted coconut off his fingers. "What's a zygote?"

Going Nowhere

"Well, okay," I said, "let's start with mitosis . . ."

Keith's chair creaked. Bolt failure seemed imminent. "Let's not."

"All right, all right," I said, holding up my paycheck. "Can you cash this for me instead?"

Keith glared. "How do I know it's good?"

I showed him the seal of Happy Video. I showed him the address of the store. I showed him his signature.

He shook his head. "Sorry, looks forged."

"Seriously," I said. "I have, like, no money."

Keith popped the register and shrugged. "We got, like, eight bucks in here. It's been deader than Mick Jagger tonight."

"Mick Jagger's alive," I said.

Keith nodded, as if that proved his point. He stood and shoved a big ham-fist into his pocket. "Here. You can borrow this."

I held out my palm. He filled it with nickels and lint.

"Wow. Great. Must be at least a dollar twenty."

"No problemo," Keith said, and popped open a Snickers.

On the way out, I picked up a couple of things off the floor and straightened a few movie boxes. At the door Keith said, "Stan?"

"Yeah?"

"Knock her socks off."

Miles pulled up fifteen minutes later. Cari was in the front seat and Ellen was waiting in the back.

Faster

"Hi," I said, sliding in.

"Hey, Stan," Cari said.

"Nice shirt, Mr. Blackwell," Miles said.

Ellen gave me a little wave that said she was still singed by her time in the Fry Mobile. She was wearing a white sweater (low-cut), jeans (tight), and makeup (lots). She looked totally different. I put off trying to decide how much I liked it or not.

"Listen, I am so, *so* sorry."

"It's okay," she said, squeezing my elbow. "Really. It took me a while to catch my breath, but . . ."

"So, you've met Chopper!" Miles said.

Ellen laughed. Miles revved the engine.

"Where we going?" I asked.

Miles looked at me in the rearview, tearing around a corner, which forced Ellen to press against my chest. She was warm and soft, two hundred twenty volts of longing shot from my ankle to my neck.

"It's a surprise!" Miles winked, and then passed another car.

A half hour later, we walked into a large, loud room. There were beer steins on all the windowsills and pictures of soccer players on the walls. The waitresses wore frilly white dresses and blue aprons. The busboys wore blue lederhosen and little hats. Plates of schnitzel and weiners and wursts came pouring out of the kitchen, carried on enormous platters to families sitting at picnic tables arrayed about the room.

"German food?" I laughed. "*German* food?"

"What?" he said. "This place is great!"

"I'm with you, Stan," Cari said, sticking out her tongue. "Ick."

"Where's your sense of adventure, huh?" Miles asked. "Plus, as an added bonus, I called ahead to make sure they don't serve tofu!"

"How about you, Ellen?" Cari asked. She was wearing a skirt and a green blouse and almost no makeup. She had little dark ringlets and dark skin that made her look always tan. She had a way of asking you questions like she really cared about the answers.

Ellen looked around, and then shrugged. "It's umm . . . interesting."

"Very diplomatic," Miles said. "Very United Nations."

"Boutros Boutros-Ghali," I said, just because it was fun to say.

There were men at the bar looking at Ellen. There were women at the bar, but none of them looked at me. A severe old man in a green suit led us to a table.

"I wonder if they've ever heard of salad," Cari said, looking at her menu.

"Amen," Ellen agreed.

"*Salad?*" Miles hissed, mock-outraged. "Shhhh . . . they'll kick us out."

Someone in the kitchen dropped a plate, punctuating his warning.

"Well, guys, what'll it be?" the waitress asked, suddenly

just *there,* large and blond and imposing. Her name tag said
BUFFY.

Buffy?

Miles ordered himself a beer. We all looked at one another while Buffy wrote it on her little pad.

"Um . . . all the way around," I said, hoping my voice
sounded a fraction deeper than usual.

"Sorry, hon," Buffy said, smacking her gum, "but I'm
gonna have to see your ID."

"Ummm . . . ," I said, looking at Ellen, who was staring
at the floor. I looked at Cari, who jutted her lip in sympathy.

"I think I . . . um . . . left it at . . ."

"Okay," Buffy said, "so that's one beer and three Diet
Cokes, right?"

I nodded lamely.

"Be right back."

Ellen was looking at Miles with a grin. "Wow. How come
they don't card you?"

Miles shrugged. "I have the mojo."

"What*ever,*" Cari said, turning to me. "I should have warned
you, Stan. Miles always does that. He gets a kick out of it."

"No, I get a *beer* out of it," Miles said, a little snappy.
They kind of glared at each other. I'd never seen Miles and Cari
argue before, not even a little.

Buffy came back with an enormous beer and three tiny
and pathetic Cokes and took our order. The girls went first, then
me and Miles.

"So," Buffy said in disbelief, staring mostly at me, "that's *three* salads and *one* bratwurst plate?" She put her hand on Miles's shoulder while saying "bratwurst." He smiled and toasted her with his beer. Buffy sniffed and walked away.

"I *like* her," he said.

"You would," Cari told him.

"So." Miles grinned, ignoring Cari and turning toward Ellen and me. "Are you guys, like, *going steady*?"

There was a silence. I squeezed my fork. Miles cackled. It occurred to me that he'd started drinking before picking us up.

"Hilarious," I said. "Really."

Cari punched his arm. "Stop it."

"Ow!" he said, sucking on the red spot where her knuckle had hit him.

"So tell us about the conservatory, Ellen," Cari said.

"Hey, Ellen," Miles overrode her question, "did you know Stan's old man is an *inventor*?"

Ellen smiled. "He is?"

I shrugged. "I guess. Not really."

"Sure he is." Miles laughed, signaling to Buffy for a refill. "The *car*?"

"Oh," Ellen said, "I didn't realize that was . . . an invention."

Cari looked at the bread sticks. I looked at the bread sticks. After a while, Buffy brought over our tray, one lone bratwurst steaming toward the ceiling.

* * * *

After the world's longest dinner, Miles went to the bathroom and Ellen went to make a phone call.

"Next time, I pick," I said.

"Yes, please," Cari agreed, with a little smile, and then looked down and played with her napkin.

"What's going on with you guys?" I asked.

"It's that obvious, huh?"

"It's different, that's for sure."

She sighed. "You know I'm going to college in a few weeks, right?"

I nodded. She was going to Ohio State. "So soon?"

"I need to find an apartment. And a job. And some friends."

"I know what you mean."

"Well, Miles knows it, too. He could have applied. He could move, or . . ." She shook her head. "But he's too busy being cool and funny and now it's, like, August, you know?"

I did know. "I'm in the same boat."

"Yeah, but with Miles, it's like it's *my* fault. You're not going to blame me too, are you?"

I laughed. For some reason, I wanted to tell her about Berkeley. About how I wasn't going. How I was way behind signing up and being hazed and buying a new sweatshirt and everything.

"By the way, why aren't you going anywhere?" she asked. "Of all people —"

"Excuse me!" I interrupted, as our waitress walked by. Buffy didn't seem to hear and kept going.

"You want me to take it up to the register?" Cari asked.

"I'll go." I smiled. "I have way more experience in this area."

"What area?"

"That'll be four ninety-eight," I said in a falsetto, "due back Wednesday."

Cari giggled. Then resumed torturing her napkin.

"But I'm not sure I have enough," I said, unbelievably glad Ellen wasn't there to see. I held up my check and showed it to Cari. "Didn't have time to cash it."

"Don't worry about it," Cari said, and gave me another twenty. "I always come prepared. Miles tends to disappear when the check arrives."

"That jerk." I smiled.

"That jerk," she said, not smiling.

I crossed the room, looking for the cashier. Busboys and waitresses crisscrossed at top speed. Families came and went, children yelling. Men sat at the bar, cursing at a soccer game. Somehow I got lost and missed the front desk completely. I took a left and almost walked into a utility closet.

"Ha-ha," said some guy, pointing at me. He had a lone strand of sauerkraut dangling from his chin.

"Yeah," said his friend, "ha."

They slapped five.

I crossed the restaurant, angling toward the bathrooms,

and ended up next to a darkened hallway. On one side was a pay phone with an OUT OF ORDER sign. There was a stack of plastic high chairs. On the opposite wall was a cigarette machine. I could see Miles's crazy hair poking out above. His back was turned, so I walked over and grabbed his arm, about to say something hilarious about German food. He looked up, surprised. Ellen was leaning against the wall beneath him. He'd been kissing her.

1. Death ray
2. Apocalypse
3. Nuclear wipeout
4. Crushed under steamroller
5. Lied to. And betrayed.

"Wow," I said quietly, suddenly clinging to a buoy in the middle of the frozen Atlantic. Icebergs bobbed and stars glittered and I was a thousand miles from the closest ship, a Liberian freighter that couldn't see me, and wouldn't have rescued me even if it could.

Ellen pushed Miles, making space to reach out. "Stan!" And then it was a blur. Miles's mouth, wide open, in an almost comical O. Someone coming down the hall. A waiter with plates and me pushing him. Everything falling. Breaking glass and rivulets of beer. Buffy closing on my flank like a sheepdog. Someone yelling "STAN!" their voice rising and farther away at the same time.

I ran through the parking lot and alongside the highway, down over the gravel edge. I clambered through a gully, mud and plants and trash, and then up the other side, over the guardrail and across three lanes, a swerving truck and a blaring horn. I didn't care. I didn't flinch. There was a screech and a howl and I held my breath, frozen in time.

Something would or wouldn't happen.

It always doesn't or does.

Treatment for the feature-length film titled
GOING NOWHERE FASTER©

Written by Stan "Tied to the Whipping Post" Smith

A modern satire! This is a story about a model named Thistle. An incredibly thin model who is world-famous, her picture on billboards and buses, magazines and commercials. Her ability to turn sideways and practically disappear nearly puts Siegfried and Roy out of business.

   Suddenly, in a bizarre twist, Thistle will appear in public extremely fat. She will have completely let go, pushing two hundred and fifty pounds. There will be a public outcry. In an episode of *Oprah*, Thistle will sit in a chair, gorging on bacon while audience members and callers revile her. She doesn't care. She gives an impassioned speech outlining the pleasures of fatness and repudiating patriarchal notions of body image. Despite the outcries of the attorney general and various religious leaders, young girls around the globe begin to embrace fatness. It becomes the hip thing to do. Fatness takes over fashion, and millions of obese girls start Web sites, found clubs, meet at malls and stuff themselves with multiple Cinnabons. Someone (my dad) invents a device called The Equalizer, endorsed by Thistle, which is a tube with a motorized pump, built in accordance with foie gras manufacturing techniques, that forces a mixture of lard and chocolate down the throat of girls while they sleep. It is astonishingly effective and sales skyrocket.

Going Nowhere

The film examines societal hypocrisy and the nature of perfection. It veers toward feminist rhetoric, but never close enough to scare away possible readers of *Details*. In the end, we realize how culpable we all are, but respect the screenwriter for not rubbing our noses in it. Negative body image is a bad thing and many young girls are scarred. We will be forced to acknowledge that there is a true beauty in all body types, just as there is a saleable script in all plots. And an excuse for all Ellens. Or not.

CHAPTER TWELVE
THE BLUE *but very talkative and lane-switching and horn-beeping* ANGEL

A powder blue Datsun screeched to a halt in the breakdown lane, burning rubber for fifty feet. A woman stepped out of the driver's side. She wore a cowboy hat and had frizzy blond hair. Cars whizzed past. A couple tooted their horns, *bee-meep,* as she clacked toward me.

"OHMYGOD, hon . . . are you okay?"

I shrugged. "Okay?" It was a many-tiered question. There was such nuance. I was breathing, sure. On the other hand, I was Stan. On the side of the highway. Was that okay? Not really, no. Ellen. Miles. Lips. Spit. None of those things were okay. Still, my feet were warm and I wasn't hungry. So it was a toss-up. Depended how metaphysical you wanted to get. Did Shiva or Allah have an opinion? One of those eight-armed monkey gods? I wasn't sure what to tell her. Or if I could tell her anything. My body was fine, though, and that's what she meant.

"Not really," I said anyhow.

"You're hurt? Where? Show me. " She grabbed my arm and lifted it. She spun me around, looking up and down. "You don't look hurt."

"Looks can be deceiving," I said. "Like, for instance, one minute someone can be your best friend. And then you see them leaning over by the stacked chairs and suddenly they're not anymore."

"Did you hit your head?" She frowned. "You sound like maybe you took one to the noggin." She felt around through my hair. "Nothing soft. Nothing wet. No bumps."

"The bumps are all on the inside," I said. I knew it sounded ridiculous, but I couldn't help it.

She gave me a smirk. "Ain't it the truth? C'mon."

I followed, wiping my eyes as we reached the circle of light coming from the pickup's cab. A little bell pinged to let me know the door was open. I suddenly completely hated that little bell.

"Get in, get in!" she said. "Are you in? Good." Her hair billowed in the wake of another truck as she closed the door. "*Ohmygod,* for a sec there? You scared me to, like, to *death.*"

I liked her Southern accent. I liked her tight jeans. She seemed really, really concerned. About me. A stranger concerned about me. It was weird. I apologized for making her stop.

"That's okay. Look, hon, where'm I taking you?"

SIX PLACES A STRANGE WOMAN WAS TAKING ME:
    1. For a ride
    2. To the cleaners

3. The distance
4. Baby, one more time
5. For a fool
6. As it comes

"Home, I guess."

"Right," she said, as we pulled back into traffic. She reached over and turned down the music, Dolly Parton busy being all peaches and cream.

"Where's home?"

"Kansas City."

"Ha!" She laughed, and punched me lightly on the arm. "No, but really."

"Millville," I said.

"Check." She swerved into the fast lane and gunned the little truck. "So whatcha doin' in the middle of the highway, anyhow?"

"Looking for arrowheads."

"*Ohmygod!*" she said, smacking herself on the forehead. "Are you running away? Yes? No? It's all right, you don't have to tell me. I did it once myself, though. Had a stepdad and couldn't stand him. My name's Daphne. What's your name? It's okay, you don't have to tell me."

"Stan?"

"You don't seem so sure about it, hon."

"Ain't it the truth?" I said, in a really bad cowboy accent. It was fun. I wanted to talk that way the rest of my life, conceivably a short one, given the way she was driving. Daphne leaned over to shake my hand. Hers was tiny and covered with silver and turquoise rings. She wore a powder blue T-shirt that said *Way To Go!* in sparkly cursive. There were fast-food wrappers and Big Gulp containers and magazines all over the floor.

"Your truck needs a wash," I said.

"Yeah, well." She laughed, all teeth. "My truck needs a lot of things. *I* need a lot of things. Wanting 'em isn't the same as having 'em, though, is it?"

"You have no idea."

She shook her head and made a little hooting sound. "'Fraid I do, hon."

FIVE ROLES DAPHNE SHOULD BE PAID MILLIONS TO PLAY:

1. The nice, perky nurse on some hospital show
2. The nice, perky clerk on some lawyer show
3. Mary Ann's perkier sister on *Gilligan's Island*
4. The big-haired chick who rescues Stan on *Charlie's Angels*
5. The nice woman who gives Stan poison at the end of *Staneo and Ellenette*

Dolly boomed and I looked out the window for a while and then for some reason went ahead and told Daphne everything. About Miles and Berkeley and Ellen at the lake and the farm and Prarash, and finally about The Kiss. Once I started, I couldn't stop. She nodded and pulled on her lip and didn't say a word until I was done.

"Oh, I'm sorry. Oh, man, really! Some girls, I swear. But some guys, too! Oh, man is *that* the truth, I can't tell you how many times I've been sitting where you are."

I looked down. "Knee-deep in wrappers in the passenger seat of a strange woman's truck?"

"Ha! No, not that, hon. You're funny, you know it? Did anyone ever tell you that? But, no, I meant luck with men. *My* kind of luck? Whew. Still, I bet that girl has no idea what a mistake she made. But some girls are like that, you know? Grass is always greener, boy is always greener, from one to another like a bumblebee. But eventually she realizes what she's missing out on, and then it's back to the hive."

"Missing out on?" She might be missing out on Miles and all the talents he could display for anyone else's girlfriend behind a cigarette machine. But me? No.

Daphne steered the truck suddenly to the right, and we roared off the Millville exit. It was the middle of summer, all the plants bursting with life. They smelled like corn and perfume and just plain green. Why couldn't I be a plant? Just grow and be happy to reach a little higher every day. Take the sun or the rain as it comes. Let my roots go a little deeper and eat my chlorophyll and stop worrying all the time. At least until fall.

"Sure she is, Stan. I can tell already. Can I tell? You bet I can. You're a catch. Maybe not so smart for walking in the middle of the highway, and a touch on the smart-alecky side, but still."

"Are you hitting on me?" I asked. "You're not, are you?"

"Ha! I don't think I'm quite your speed, hon."

"That's good," I said. "I wasn't sure I'd be able to let you down easy."

She smiled. I wiped my eyes with my T-shirt as Daphne pulled up in front of my parents' house.

"Weird," she said. "Is this your house? Is this *a* house?"

"Yeah, my dad built it."

"With what?" Daphne asked.

"Umm . . . wood?" I guessed.

"*Ohmygod,* that was so *rude,*" she said. "I am so sorry."

"So am I," I said. "Anyway, I really appreciate the ride." I reached into my pocket and pulled out a crumpled dollar. "Here's for gas."

Daphne shooed the bill away. "You keep that, honey. You'll give someone else a good turn. It all equals out somewhere along the line. And don't you worry about that girl. The world's full of girls. Am I right? You bet I am."

Daphne waved and pulled away with a squeal.

It was dark and hot.

I crunched up gravel toward the house, as dark and scary and crickety as ever. The shadows had shadows and the grass was wet and humid and there was a sinister hum in the air. My heart pounded as I felt my way around back, past the hut and the gooseberry furrows and the rusting tractor. An old pitchfork lay in the dirt, practically frowning. I picked it up and leaned it against the porch. Since the porch leaned too, it slid and fell again. There was something seriously wrong with the world. Like someone went back in time to check out the dinosaurs and stepped on a butterfly by mistake and that dead butterfly started a chain reaction where fifty million years later we all had tails. Or kissed our best friend's girlfriends. Bradbury could go screw, too.

I climbed the steps two at a time, but slowly, adjusting for the lean. *Two, four, six, eight, ten.* It felt good to count. Counting was comforting. *Twelve, fourteen,* door.

Safe.

Except for the thing that was waiting on the top step. In the corner. From a shadow, one eye peered.

"Hello?" I said, like a moron.

No answer.

I stepped closer.

"Chopper?"

No answer. I held my breath and leaned over.

It was one of Olivia's dolls.

"Oh, man," I said, exhaling with relief. Until I noticed it was painted red.

Bright red.

All over, from toes to hair.

Even the pupils.

Plus, across the forehead, written in black, was a name. My name. STAN. I dropped the doll. I almost screamed. And then I did.

All the house lights were off. I was seeing double, sweat

Going Nowhere

in my eyes. I slammed the door behind me and ran up the stairs, not even feeling the cracks against my shins. I found my room and crawled into bed and climbed under the covers, pulling them tight and trying really, really hard not to scream again.

CHAPTER THIRTEEN
THE *bedridden and not worthy of it*
SHAWSHANK *and foot-stank* REDEMPTION

MONDAY: "Stan? Honey? Are you getting up?"

I wasn't. I decided, first thing after opening my eyes, I was permanently on strike from life. All I needed was a bullhorn and a placard. I could walk in front of the house and yell slogans and blow whistles and pretend to be upset about animal rights. Or Stan's rights. "WHAT DO WE WANT? SLEEP! WHEN DO WE WANT IT? NOW!" No, that's not enough. Not nearly enough scope. It had to be the rights of Stans *around the world* to never get out of bed! We were all in it together. Me and my fellow misnamed. We could have demands:

1. Anyone named Miles immediately chopped up and bagged and shipped halfway across the planet to be used as mulch in someone's garden.
2. All four Beatles kidnapped or revived and forced to go into the studio to record a new song called "Eleanor Pigby."
3.

So, I guess we only needed two demands.

I was enjoying the possibilities when the doorknob ratcheted back and forth. It pushed and pulled. "Stan? Stanley?"

I pulled the covers over my head and the sheet over my head and the pillow over my head. It was warm and quiet despite the muffles and the ratcheting. Then, just before falling asleep, I heard my father say, "Leave him alone."

Good ol' Dad.

TUESDAY: "STAN! Keith is on the phone? Aren't you going to work? Stan?"

I wasn't. I hadn't eaten in twenty-four hours and it felt good. It felt ascetic, like a monk or a yogi. It hurt a little, but in the right way. I was paying my dues. I was cleansing and purifying. I was lying under my covers and rubbing my feet together, the time-worn method of holy sufferers everywhere, quietly reminding ourselves of our mortality. And our lack of socks. Maybe, when the time came, not eating was something I could talk Keith into.

KEITH'S NEW MENU OPTIONS:
1. Water
2. Sprouts
3. Sprout-water
4. Half-washed yam
5. Dirty yam

Of course, that's if I ever saw him again. I wasn't even getting up for socks, and Happy Video was way across town. So the math was against it. Maybe, in a month or so, he'd visit me bedside. Maybe he'd come in with a canvas tunic and a crown of laurel and splash me with lavender water. Isn't that what they did with martyrs? Or did they burn them over a pile of Dura-flames? Either way, I wasn't going to work.

WEDNESDAY: "Listen, Stan, this is ridiculous! You *have* to get out of bed. Really. I called Dr. Felder. He says you *have* to get out of bed."

But I didn't. Have to. At all. It was revelatory. It was amazing. Day three, and it just kept getting better. It wasn't like one of those things you thought when you were little, like maybe you could poke your plastic shovel into the sand and dig a hole to China, but only got a foot down before the ocean poured in and destroyed your hard work and swept your sand away. And your hopes and your girlfriend. And who really wanted to go to China anyhow? Who wanted to go anywhere, for that matter? We all had beds, didn't we? Give me a round-trip ticket to my Serta Sleeper. Give me a six-day, seven-night all expenses paid trip to my duck-feather comforter. Plus, there was the doll. Okay, I admit it. It scared me to death. It might still be on the doorstep. Or, standing in the hallway. Waiting.

I wasn't going anywhere.

THURSDAY: Olivia whispered through the keyhole, "Stanny?"

And that, finally, was what it took. Plus, I was starving. I was dreaming my pillow was a cannoli. It was covered with drool. Also, my back hurt and I stank. Olivia didn't say anything, just climbed onto the bed and curled up at my feet like a cat. She was carrying a doll. I almost screamed, but it was just a normal doll. Not red. Not painted. Not with my name on the forehead.

"You okay?" she asked.

"Yeah," I said, looking at the doll again. Double check. Triple check. It looked back at me with a tiny plastic smile. "Everything's great."

"There's something wrong with you and Ellen, isn't there?"

"What makes you think that?"

Olivia shrugged. Her little chin was turned up and her eyes were sad and brown and I felt bad for making her concerned.

"Everything's okay. Really."

"You don't have to lie, Stanny," she said. She held my foot like a pillow and closed her eyes and we napped together. I had another dream. I was running on the beach and someone was following me with a stick and they kept hitting me with it every time I told them that I hated when people told me about their dreams.

When I woke up, Olivia was gone. My mother was back. The door was open. She sat in the tiny divot where Olivia had been, like time-lapse photography. Scary.

"Mom . . . ," I began, but she held up her hand. She played with her big hoop earring for a while and then took a deep breath and said, "Your father tells me I embarrassed you. Certainly I didn't *mean* to, and frankly I still don't understand how, but I will say that I am very, very sorry."

"It's okay," I said, tucking my chin near my armpit. I could smell myself. The long crinkly and reasonably new hairs under my arm, acrid and oily but not entirely unpleasant. It made me uncomfortable to be sniffing my armpit with my mother so close, though, so I stopped.

"No, Stan," she said, "it's *not* okay."

"Yes, Mom," I said, desperately wanting her to go away, "it *is*."

She shook her head and I knew she was thinking of some phrase she'd seen on a talk show or read about in a book on the woes of dealing with teenagers, or something Dr. Felder told her, like, *When they're difficult, take a deep breath and really try to FEEL where they're coming from.* Still, I didn't want her to get mad and I didn't want to waste the small advantage of being apologized to, so I went ahead and explained.

"Ellen? Eleanor? And me. It's over. Before it even started. So the whole thing? With the car? It doesn't make any difference."

"Is *that* what all this is about?" My mother shook her head. "I thought this was about Berkeley."

Berkeley. I'd forgotten all about it.

"Yeah, what about that?" I said. "All of a sudden I'm accepted to some school? That I didn't even apply to?"

"I know, Stan. It's just . . ."

"It's just what?"

She took a deep breath and exhaled slowly. She played with her skirt, which had elephants and giraffes running across it, followed by cartoon poachers. "By going there, you have a chance to finish what I started. Can you understand that?"

"But I don't want to go to Berkeley. I want to make a movie. I want to *write* a movie."

She frowned. "You do?"

"I think."

"I'm not sure that's the smartest idea I've ever heard, Stan."

"Why not?"

"Well, for one thing, it's something you can easily do *after* college. Besides, why haven't you ever said anything about it before? Here I am driving you to the chess clubs and the dinosaur clubs and the math clubs and the algebra addicts, but never once anything about a script?"

"I work at a video store, Mom," I said. "I watch about twelve movies a day."

She sighed. "True. It's just . . ."

"It's just what?"

"After the whole thing with your uncle Stu? "

Uncle Stu was my mother's brother. He was also small and dull and smoked long cigarettes that smelled like burnt cat.

"What about him?"

"Well, I assumed your father had told you. His script? I thought that's where this was coming from."

"Uncle Stu wrote a *script*? I thought he was retired."

"Well, he is," my mother said, shaking her head. "At least as a dentist. He somehow got a patient to show his script to their cousin in exchange for a bridge and two crowns. That cousin was an agent and apparently loved it. So Stu moved to Hollywood. He lived there for three years, but the movie was never made."

"Then what?"

"Well, as you know, your uncle is now very wealthy and living in Hawaii."

"Did he sell his gold tooth collection?"

"No, he won a lawsuit."

"What kind of lawsuit?"

My mother sighed deeply. "Well, his script was about a prison. A women's prison."

"Why didn't *I* think of that?" I said, slapping my forehead.

"Yes, well, this movie that was never made was called *Prison Girrlz.* It seems some rapper's group stole the name and put it on their records and Stu sued them. For a lot. Of money."

"*Rapper's* group?" I said, laughing. "*Prison* Girls?"

"Two *R*'s and a *Z*," my mother said.

"No way!"

"Yes way."

I couldn't believe it. Just when my family was at its absolute quota of maximum weirdness. Olivia yelled "Mom!" from downstairs. Then she did it three more times, "MOM-MOMMOM!"

My mother got up. "We can talk more about this later. But for now, why don't you go take a shower?" She held her nose and made a face. "Or two showers? And I'll make you something to eat. And then call Keith. You're late for work. And call Miles. He called about twenty-six times. And call Dr. Felder. You missed your appointment. He said you were 'off the hook,' whatever that means."

"Okay," I said.

As she stepped out the door I suddenly remembered the message on the back steps. Somehow I'd refused to think about it. For even a second. "Mom, did you find a doll outside?"

She looked in at me. "No, why?"

"A red doll? Like, a scary one?"

"Take a shower, Stanley," she said, walking down the stairs.

I threw the covers on the floor and got up for the first time in a week. It was like being born. Again.

CHAPTER FOURTEEN
RAGING *actually pretty calm but probably hungry and not at all happy* **BULL**

I rode into town an hour early, feeling like I owed Keith for missing (at least) two shifts. I figured I'd make it up to him by explaining the advantages of his new sprout-water diet.

I locked my bike to the Dumpster and then walked in the front door. The lights were off and Keith was standing in the middle of the store talking to a policeman, who was taking Felder-ish notes in his pad. Video cases were all over the carpet. Ceiling tiles hung at odd angles, and wiring was pulled down and exposed. There was broken glass and broken video equipment and posters torn in long strips. The register was on its side, yanked open like an oyster. Hundreds of pennies were strewn across the floor. The word "nats" was spray-painted all over the walls in red. NATSNATSNATSNATS. It was everywhere, impossible to keep your eyes off of. Had the store been robbed? It'd definitely been trashed. It was unbelievable.

"What's going on?" I asked. NATS.

Keith stared at me for a minute and then picked an Almond Joy from the rubble and stuck it in his mouth.

"Careful," I said, unable to stop myself, "that could be evidence."

Keith didn't laugh. I didn't blame him. I knew it wasn't funny, but I didn't know what else to say.

"Sorry."

"Where you been, Stan?" Keith asked.

The cop looked me over, squinting. "*This* is Stan?"

Keith nodded, his enormous perm even more enormous than usual. "Yup, that's him."

"Where you been, Stan?" the cop asked, writing in his pad. NATS. He looked familiar and it took me a minute to place him. Dave Munter. He was the older brother of a kid in my class and had been out of high school for a few years. He'd been picked on a lot (join the club). Even now, when his car drove by the school, everyone would yell and whistle and laugh. He was not a friendly guy.

"What are you writing?"

"I asked you a question," Officer Dave said. He was thin, with a thin mustache and thin, angry eyes. He wore shorts and his knobby legs were sunburned. He had about eight thousand pounds of equipment on his belt and mirrored sunglasses pushed on top of his head. He chewed gum with an accusing snap.

FIVE POSSIBLY MORE ACCURATE NICKNAMES FOR OFFICER DAVE:

1. Officer Jane

2. Mr. Burn and Peel
3. Pee Jay Hooker
4. Captain Kneesocks
5. The Angry Inch

"Um . . . ," I said, stalling. What could I tell them? Where *had* I been? I couldn't really say that I'd refused to get out of bed for a week. I couldn't say I'd joined the Brotherhood of the Sheet. NATS.

"I've . . . uh . . . been sick," I said.

"Sick," Keith said.

"Sick," Officer Dave repeated, chomping his gum. He wrote something in his pad.

"That's not what your mom said." Keith peeled open another candy bar and offered it to Officer Dave, who shook his head without taking his eyes off me. Keith swallowed it in one bite.

"My mom?"

"Yeah, your mom. When I talked to her on Monday. And Tuesday. And Wednesday. Days you were supposed to work. Days she said you were just in bed. Lying there. Like you were feeling too guilty to get up."

I was sweating. NATS. There was a knot in my stomach. NATS. There was no sign of my friend Keith inside this large angry man. There was no smile there at all.

"Sorry," I said again.

Keith threw an empty *The Way We Were* box on the ground. "Why would someone do this? To my store? Sure, steal the cash, whatever. You know what they got away with?" He was staring at me. "About fifty bucks."

Officer Dave nodded sympathetically.

"But then why trash it? *Why?*"

"Drugs," said Officer Dave. He pointed his thumb in my direction, like I wasn't even there. "These kids?" He shrugged and flipped his pad closed, as if it completed his thought. "And what's with this NATS business?"

"Yeah, Stan," Keith asked. NATS. "Do you know what that's all about?"

"I bet it's some new drug," Officer Dave said.

I swallowed hard. It was like the old eye-cue test all over again. "Um . . . I guess it's STAN backward?"

Keith looked at Officer Dave. Officer Dave nodded and then looked at me slyly. "Very smart. Use your own name to throw us off the scent? Wow. That's what we police call advanced criminal thinking."

"What scent?" I said. "Keith?"

"No one's accusing anyone of anything," Officer Dave said. "Yet."

I wiped my neck and then my forehead. I couldn't believe it.

"Listen," I said. "Okay, the other night I come home and there's this doll, right? A red doll that —"

"A red doll?" Officer Dave said, smirking at Keith. Keith shook his head and wiped nougat off his mustache. Officer Dave didn't write "red" or "doll" in his little pad.

"Okay, forget that," I said. "Someone tried to run me over. In their car? Like, I was riding my bike and —"

"Run you over?" Officer Dave said, rolling his eyes. "You look okay to me."

It was hopeless. Why was I even bothering? They stared, like Laurel and Hardy. Except Hardy was big and mean and wanted to eat my leg for lunch. Laurel was skinny and weird and wore his socks way too high.

"Chad Chilton," I said, but they didn't even hear. I dabbed my underarm with a copy of *The Accused.* Jodie Foster's nose soaked in my sweat. "Umm . . . I know this is a dumb question, but, do you need me to work my shift?"

Keith laughed. Officer Dave laughed.

"Work your shift, Stan?" Keith said. "Maybe you should try looking around."

"Happy Video is now a crime scene," Officer Dave said.

"Happy Video is now officially closed," Keith said. "Even if you weren't fired. Which you are." He kicked some boxes out of his way and turned and walked back into what was left of his office.

"Don't leave town," Officer Dave warned, then left himself.

Outside, my bike had two new flats. Both tires had long horizontal slashes across them, ugly jagged rips that looked like they were made with someone's teeth. I looked around. The parking lot was empty. No traffic, no kids, no birds, nothing. What was going *on*? I unlocked the bike and walked it alongside me. *Fired?* Fired. From Happy Video. It was like being fired from breathing. How could Keith look at me that way? Blank, like a fish. Did he really think I had anything to do with robbing the store? Could things possibly get any worse?

It took me an hour to walk home. My mother was downstairs, laughing. I could hear Prarash's voice. Olivia was taking a nap and my father was somewhere in the bowels of the house banging metal together. I made a peanut butter (organic and hard as a rock) sandwich and carried it up to my room, where it sat on the bookshelf until I fell asleep.

In the morning, my mother popped her head in the door. It was early, not even six. I sat up, mentally preparing to wash yams.

"Let me guess. Prarash is late?"

Her face was ashy and scared. For a second I was positive there was something wrong with Olivia.

"No, Stan," my mother said. "I just got a call from Sheriff Conner. Roberto was arrested last night."

"*Arrested*? Which one?"

"Dos."

"But why?"

"I don't know yet," she said, and left the door open, as if there were nothing else to ask. I sat up and quickly got dressed. I was going to have to walk into town. Or wheel my bike, which was the same thing as walking, except with a bike next to you. I couldn't call Miles. I couldn't talk to Ellen. Keith hated my guts. Olivia was too small to understand. I considered talking to myself in the mirror, but it was just too much like *Risky Business.* Chopper nosed his way in and watched me tie my shoes. He wagged his little nub tail and drooled on my carpet.

"What should I do, buddy?"

"Woof," he answered, which was really no answer at all.

Treatment for the feature-length film entitled
GOING NOWHERE FASTER©

Written by Stan "Kid Savage" Smith

This is a movie about a superhero named Roy. In real life
he's a mild-mannered race starter. Yup, Roy's the guy who
shoots the cap gun and then all the guys bounce out of
their crouches and start zooming toward the hurdles, or
whatever. Nobody notices Roy unless he screws up, like
shoots his cap gun too soon, and then everyone boos. Anyway,
one night Roy is walking home from the racetrack and falls
into a pile of radioactive waste. Or no, he sees a lost puppy
out on the test range, and runs out to rescue him just before
the Evil General okays a strontium bomb experiment. Either
way, it gives Roy special powers. He wakes up that night
feeling strong. He climbs the walls and walks on the ceiling
and does an uneven-bar routine on his shower rod. Then he
sews himself a really tight lycra suit and becomes Margin-
ally Effective Deterrent Man. See, the blast at the test
range gave him powers, just not enough powers. He keeps
trying to stop crime, but never stops it quite enough. He
shows up at the bank robbery and manages to turn off the
alarm that's hurting everyone's ears, but the robbers still
get away with the cash. He stops a couple from being mugged
on their way home from the theatre, but only manages to
recover one diamond earring, and not the wallet or tie pin
or pocketbook the mugger ran off with. He manages to give
the city's crime boss a whole lot to worry about, like spam-
ming his computer and breaking the windshield wipers off
his Hummer and sticking a potato in his drainpipe so his

Faster

basement floods, but really doesn't do much about the crime boss's citywide reign of terror. Also, the red-headed intrepid female reporter that Roy is in love with thinks he's kind of a jerk. And ignores him. And then the credits roll. And the whole thing about the huge meteor that's about to crash into Earth is never really addressed. Or maybe Roy is like "Run! Run!" and some people do, but, on the other hand, others don't. And it's ironic he's telling people to run, being a racetrack starter guy and all.

Sigh.

CHAPTER FIFTEEN
THE *really not all that* BAD, *okay, maybe that bad* SEED

Sheriff Conner had bright red bangs and a huge potbelly. He had bright red sideburns and a bright red mustache and bright red hair on his arms. He looked up from his desk when I walked in the door and smiled. He'd been really nice to me about the whole burning-locker thing.

"Stan! Hey, buddy."

"Hi, Sheriff."

He was also a big chess fan. We'd played a game or two while waiting for my mother to pick me up. Or maybe we'd been waiting for Chad Chilton to decline to press charges. Either way, he kicked out a plastic chair, so I sat on the other side of his desk.

"Game?"

"Why not?"

He pulled out a chessboard, the kind that folded in half and had Chinese checkers on the back. There were two pieces missing, a bottle-cap rook and a lighter-knight. Sheriff Conner held out his hands and I picked the left one. It opened to reveal a white pawn. He set it in front of me and started arranging his black pieces. I moved my queen's pawn ahead two spaces.

"Listen, Sheriff, you need to let Dos go."

"Who?" he asked, countering with his own queen's pawn. I pushed ahead my bishop's pawn two spaces, attacking it.

"Roberto."

Sheriff Conner frowned. He concentrated by squeezing one of his ears, which had little red hairs coming out of it. He let out a long sigh before deciding to take my pawn, which was a mistake, then looked up and said, "Sorry, Stan, no can do. We caught him red-handed. Found traces of rutabaga seed all over the video store. Same seed your mom says you use in planting. Only farm in a hundred miles uses that seed. Found those seeds in Roberto's shoes. Slam dunk."

"Why were you looking at his shoes? Isn't that kind of random?"

"Anonymous tipster."

I slid my knight in front of his pawn, blocking it, a simple ruse. Make him think he was ahead and waste time protecting a piece out of place to begin with. His hand hovered over the board, unsure. It was weird how obvious it was, and that, somehow, it wasn't clear to him. I almost wanted to yell, *Don't!* He took the bait and sat back, satisfied.

"But that's crazy. Dos would never do anything like that."

"No one ever thinks so, but people keep doing crazy things. Plus, it took me three tries to arrest the right one. Who knew there were three Robertos? Not big on names in that family, huh?"

"True," I said, "but I practically almost know who really did it."

Sheriff Conner raised an eyebrow. "You do?"

"It was Chad Chilton. He's been chasing me around, doing weird stuff. I know it was him."

"Chilton, huh?" Sheriff Conner snorted. "Young guy? Muscle car? I think I played football with his father."

"Anyway, since now you know who it was, can you let Roberto go?"

"Isn't this Chilton the one whose locker you lit up?"

I gulped, doomed. "Um, yeah, but this has nothing to do with that. Or maybe everything. I dunno. But there was a red doll on my doorstep! And then my bike tires? And the spray-painting? And then, the last day of school he's like 'I'll get you.' Or whatever."

Sheriff Conner nodded, stroking his leg and staring at the board. "Is it my move?"

"Yes. So are you going to arrest Chad Chilton?"

"No, I'm not, Stan. Doesn't sound like any real solid evidence to me. Sounds like a movie, actually. And not a very good one."

He was right. I sounded like an idiot.

FIVE GREAT TITLES FOR A PRISON MOVIE:
1. *The Heartburn Motel*
2. *Digging to Mexico One Spork at a Time*

Faster

"Well, can I at least go see Roberto?"

Sheriff Conner didn't answer, coming to terms with the hopelessness of his position. Finally, he conceded the game. "I lasted longer than the last one though, huh?"

I nodded. "Can I see Dos, Sheriff?"

He rubbed his beard. "I'm not supposed to let you, Stan."

I looked at him but didn't say anything, waiting. I already knew he would let me, just like I knew he would take my baited pawn. He finally nodded and said, "Okay, five minutes. And *no* telling your mother."

"Deal," I said.

The cell was like something from the *Dukes of Hazzard*. I kept expecting Cletus to pop out and ask me for a swig of rye. Dos was in a cell with one other man who appeared to be sleeping. Or passed out. Or dead.

"*Dios mio,* Stan, I so glad to see you."

"Me, too, buddy," I said, gripping Dos's shoulders through the bars. "Are you okay?"

"*Sí, sí.* No problem." He stuck out his tongue. "But the food? She is terrible."

"I'm gonna get you out of here."

"Okay. Good."

"But listen, I have to ask you something, okay? Don't get mad."

Dos nodded.

"You didn't do it, did you? The store?"

"Qué?"

"Tu no estás the robber? No?"

Dos's eyes widened. He looked at me with disbelief. "NO!"

I studied him for a moment and then smiled. I couldn't believe I'd actually considered, even for a second, that he might have robbed Happy Video. Dos laughed, and I laughed with him. It was so completely stupid. "I'll see if Mrs. Dos can bring some food in," I said. "The sheriff's a nice guy, but I still kinda doubt it."

Dos reached through the bars and shook my hand solemnly.

"Another game?" Sheriff Conner asked, as I walked past his desk.

"Sorry, Sheriff, I gotta go."

He looked disappointed and began putting the pieces away.

"Listen, Sheriff, can Dos's wife bring some food in? He says the food here's terrible."

Sheriff Conner gave me a dour look. "You know my wife makes the food here, right?"

"Oh," I said, "sorry."

"You better be," he said. "Betty's a great cook."

I had to think of something quick.

"So how's Officer Dave working out?"

Sheriff Conner rolled his eyes and then cleared his throat.

"I thought so," I said, walking to the door.

"Stan?"

"Yeah?"

"You didn't have anything to do with it, did you?"

I opened my mouth. It just stayed there. Open.

"I hope not, Stan, 'cause if you did, we'll find out."

To be honest, I hadn't really considered that before. Had I done it? Was I losing my mind? Did I spray-paint "NATS" all over the wall as a pathetic cry for help? I reached up and closed my mouth with two fingers, like Daffy after Bugs had given him a face full of shotgun.

"No, Sheriff, I did not rob Happy Video."

"Good," he said. "By the way, heard anything about college?"

"No," I said, shaking my head.

"Smart kid like you?"

"Smart kid like me."

"Well, don't worry about it," he said. "Anyone plays chess like you do? There's always a career in criminal justice."

Next to the police station was a bakery. As I wheeled my bike through the lot (cut tires going *flop flop flop*), Prarash backed out the door with an enormous box of pastries in his arms, different kinds, all of them with some variant of frosting or cream or Boston whip. Not a single one vegan. Or organic.

"Stanley, my friend," he said, managing to smile through his beard and at the same time be completely unfriendly. It was actually a pretty impressive skill.

"How you doing, Fred?" I asked. I'd decided I was never

going to call him "Prarash" again. He was a Fred, completely and thoroughly.

Fred showed me his gums. His robe billowed in the breeze. "A young bee without manners is like a thin leaf upon which no rain can collect."

"I've been called worse things than a thin leaf," I said. "Or a young bee."

Prarash grabbed me by the wrist, hard, and squeezed. It hurt. Bad. He leaned close, eyes bloodshot and breath like tobacco, and hissed, "You still want to call me Fred? Are you sure? Or maybe are you suddenly *very* sorry?"

I tried to pull away, but couldn't. Prarash sneered. I looked around. The police station door was closed. Women talked and laughed inside the bakery, waiting in line, twenty feet away. All the cars in the lot were empty. I was scared. Prarash smelled like a wet dog.

"Yes," I said.

He shook his head. His long hair wavered. It was the closest I'd ever been to him. I noticed, for the first time, that he had hair plugs.

"Not good enough, Stanley." He grinned. "The young bee must say he's sorry."

I gritted my teeth, trying to hold out. He squeezed harder. My wrist felt like the bones were fusing together, white hot. I felt a tear in the corner of my eye.

WRIST PAIN EQUIVALENT TO:
1. Nose on fire

2. Snapped in three pieces
3. Bit by rabid lizard
4. Revenge of cranky Buddha
5. Ate three times too much ham

"Okay, okay, I'm sorry."

Prarash let go. He smiled again. "That's better." He picked up the pastry box and held it toward me. "Want one?"

I stared at him, rubbing my wrist. "No."

"In the end, we must all suit ourselves," he said, as Mrs. Thompson, the librarian, came out of the bakery. "Well, hello!" Prarash said, walking over. The two started chatting. I got on my bike and after two pedals almost crashed. Were the tires still flat? You bet. Moron. I got off and walked the bike beside me, like a wounded lamb.

CHAPTER SIXTEEN
THE MAN *actually "man" might be a slight exaggeration* **WHO KNEW** *actually very little* **TOO MUCH**

I *flop flop flopped* over to Dr. Felder's office, about to knock, but his door was already open. He had his loafers up on the desk, eating a sandwich and reading a Superboy comic. Simon and Garfunkel played softly in the background.

"Doc?"

"Stan!" he said, surprised, abruptly lowering his feet and wiping his mouth. He snapped off the radio, causing the sandwich to roll across his chest and onto the carpet, landing face-first. Dr. Felder picked it up carefully, dabbing at the stain with an already mustardy napkin, which just made it worse.

"I know I don't have an appointment, Doc, but my mother said you called, so I decided to drop in."

"Glad you did, there, Stan," he said, sliding the comic into a drawer. "Hecka glad."

I plopped onto the couch. "Hella."

"Excuse me?"

"Nothing."

"What's wrong with your wrist?" he asked, trying with the corner of a lined yellow pad to get at a piece of sandwich stuck between his teeth.

"What do you mean?"

"Well," he said, pointing, "it looks swollen. And also, you've been rubbing it ever since you got here."

I looked down. He was right. I put my hands in my pockets.

"It's fine," I said. "Bike accident."

Dr. Felder scribbled furiously in his pad, which was no longer being used for floss.

"What are you writing?"

He ignored my question. "Okay, so how's it going otherwise?"

"Not so good," I said. I'd never told him a word about Ellen and I didn't intend to start now. Besides, there was so much else horrible going on, it wasn't like we'd be lacking subjects. "Okay, first thing? My friend Dos has been arrested. I don't know what to do."

"Arrested?" Dr. Felder said in his concerned/startled voice. "For what?"

"Happy Video was broken into the other night," I said. "They think he did it."

"Hmm . . . ," Dr Felder said, chewing his pencil, "hmmm . . ."

"And I, like, know for a fact he didn't. There is something seriously wrong going on here. Like, for one thing —"

Dr. Felder scratched his nose thoughtfully. "The only

way you could know that for a *fact,* Stan, is if you were the one who did it yourself."

"Yeah," I said. "Ha-ha. Anyway, there was this red doll, and . . ."

Dr. Felder adjusted his sweater and squinted at me. After a while I realized he wasn't joking.

"Me? Are you kidding, Doc? I mean, do you really think I would . . ."

"Well, there was the locker incident," he said, about to reel off some other examples, except there weren't any others.

"How long have I been coming here, Doc?" I asked. Did I really have to explain the locker thing again? How many roads must a man push a bike with slashed tires down, before you could call him a man?

"Umm . . . a year?"

"So haven't you been *listening*?"

Dr. Felder was taken aback. He stuttered, trying to form a response. I stood up, the lyrics to "Feelin' Groovy" swelling in my head.

"Wait a minute, Stan."

"I'll let you get back to Superboy, Doc," I said. "By the way, you've got mustard on your chin."

When he looked down, I closed the door.

I got on my bike and made it about a hundred feet before the rubber started to go. Another fifty and the tires peeled off completely, rims bare and really starting to spark. And then bend. I was about a mile from Dr. Felder's office, pedaling on ovals, when Miles pulled up alongside me. It was hard to steer and almost impossible to keep from falling over. It was like whipping across a sheet of ice on skates made of celery. Somehow I managed.

"Stan!"

I ignored him. The wheels screeched and wobbled.

"*Please* pull over, huh, Amelia Earhart? We have to talk."

I skidded down a handicap ramp, catching some air. When I landed, the spokes began to snap. If I got through fast enough, I could cut behind the deli and avoid Miles completely. I just didn't get through fast enough. The front tire collapsed and I almost crashed. Miles was waiting at the bottom, arms crossed, his car awkwardly parked in the gravel lot. He stood, silhouetted by the headlights.

I lifted my bike and threw it as far as I could, which was about three feet. It made an incredible clanging noise and lay there wheezing.

"I think you might need some new tires," Miles said.

I walked toward him. When it seemed close enough, I closed my eyes and swung, hard as I could. My fist crashed into his nose. It was the first time I'd punched someone in my entire life. It felt good.

"Hey!" he said, and I swung again, missing. He charged, grabbing me around the waist. We fell to the dirt and rolled around, breathing loudly. I hit him and he hit me. Rocks poked into my back. My elbows scraped along the ground. I didn't feel any of it. Finally, exhausted, we just sort of stopped. I rolled away, wiping my eye with my shirt. I could already feel a welt coming up. Miles held his nose, blood coming from between his fingers.

"You feel better?" he asked.

"Maybe," I said. "A little."

"I think my nose is broken," he said.

"Good."

My fist was swollen. My knuckles throbbed. I was surprised that it hurt to punch someone almost as much as it did to get punched. So all that stuff in the movies was a lie, too. Flying kicks and roundhouse punches and Tom Cruise beating up an entire room of bad guys all five feet taller than him. Also, now my Prarash-wrist had company.

Miles sniffed. Blood ran from his nose and dried in the dust. Part of me wanted to help him up. The other part wanted to hit him again, but probably not without some sort of glove on.

"I am so, so sorry," he said, rubbing the knees of his corduroys with his palms.

"You are, huh? *Sorry?*" I kicked my bike. Now my toe hurt, too. "What good does sorry do me?"

"You don't understand," he said.

"What's to understand? You're supposed to be my friend. How *could* you?"

"I don't know," he said, shaking his head. "I just . . . I dunno. Somehow I got drunk . . . and really jealous."

"JEALOUS? Of what?"

"Of you."

"Of me?" I said, and then, ridiculously, said it again. "Of me?"

"YEAH, you," he yelled, suddenly angry. "You idiot! You act like everyone should feel bad for you all the time, like you've got it so hard. You don't have it hard. You're smarter than any six of us put together. You could do anything you wanted, but you're too pussy to go out on a limb and *choose.*"

"I have gone out on a limb," I said quietly. "It's just that the thing I chose didn't choose me back."

Miles nodded, rubbing his cheek.

"Besides," I said, "what about you? You have everything. The cool hair and the girl. And the convincing line of shit."

"I don't have anything," he said.

"What about Cari?"

Miles half laughed, half choked. "Cari's going to college in Ohio, or weren't you paying attention to that, either? I don't *have* her. She's leaving in two weeks. Plus, now she won't talk to me. After you ran out of the restaurant like Forrest Gump, I had to tell her what happened."

"That was smart."

"I've called her, like, forty times. She won't come to the phone. Her mom says she doesn't want to talk to me."

"That sounds familiar. Oh, well. Time for a new girl-friend, I guess."

He shook his head and wiped dirty hands through his hair. Cars whizzed by. Someone laid on their horn suggestively, *bip bip beep!* I had a strong sense of déjà vu. Then I thought about what Daphne had said in her little blue truck, about how things came around and maybe I'd be in a position sometime to help somebody else. What she hadn't said was what to do if this somebody else happened to try to steal your girlfriend.

"But I don't want a new girlfriend."

"Except Ellen," I said.

Miles spit some blood. He examined the inside of his lip. "I know you're not going to believe this, okay, but she grabbed me. I thought it was just a joke. I mean, sure, I was flirting, but I wasn't gonna *kiss* her or anything. I guess I just wanted her to like me too, and then she plants one on me. I swear, I was, like, pulling away when you walked up. I was more surprised than you were."

"Unlikely," I said.

"I swear to God, Stan, that girl is not who you think she is. If you ever believed one word out of me your whole life: *She. Kissed. Me.*"

I rubbed my elbow, which only made it hurt more. The thing was, I believed him. There was blood on the front of his shirt. I stepped over and helped him up. He limped around to the driver's side and got into his car. "You want a ride?"

"No," I said, and then noticed, in the backseat, four skateboard videos. Could it have been? Not possible.

"Where did you get those?" I snapped.

"What?"

"Those videos."

"What do you mean, where?" Miles laughed. "I rented them. At Happy Video."

"NATS," I said.

He cocked an eyebrow, confused, waiting for me to explain the joke. He waited a long time.

"Never mind." I got on my bike. It sagged and groaned. I got back off and started walking. Miles revved the engine, and then stopped.

"So are we still friends, or what?"

"I don't know," I said, rubbing my knuckles as he slowly pulled away. "I have to think about it."

CHAPTER SEVENTEEN
SATURDAY NIGHT *all night, with a high fever* FEVER

The next morning I got up before six and found my dad in the backyard. I was determined that today, maybe the first day ever, wasn't going to be all about Stan. Every other day had been so far, and look where it'd gotten us.

"Dad? I need your help with something. There's something we have to do, and it's really, really important."

"Well, I'm watching your sister at the moment," he said, tapping his chin with a wrench. "Among other things."

"That's okay," I said, "because she's coming, too."

My father sighed. "Where is this really important thing, Stan?"

I took him by the hand and led him toward the Fry-O-Lator. "You'll see."

"Does this really important thing have something to do with your bruised face and the cuts on your elbows and your swollen wrist?"

"No," I said.

"If I ask where they came from, are you going to tell me the truth?"

"Probably not."

He nodded and allowed himself to be led along.

Chopper and Olivia rolled out of the car first. I got the brushes and brooms and mops and water buckets out of the trunk. My father carried in his tools and began untying materials from the ski rack. I unlocked the back door with a key hidden in the fake rock behind the Dumpster, and set everything down in the center of the carpet.

"So this is Handy Video?" my father said, dragging in a piece of Sheetrock. It was strange he'd never been here. On the other hand, he hated movies and he hated stores, so maybe not.

"Happy," I said.

"Huh?"

"*Happy* Video, Dad," Olivia said. Chopper farted.

"Right." My father pulled out a tape measure, marking a distance six feet away from Chopper. When he was out of drift range, he began sorting lumber. Olivia picked up a stack of videos and began to alphabetize them. I grabbed a hammer.

"What does 'NATS' mean?" my father asked.

"What does 'NATS' mean?" Olivia asked.

"It means Never Aim Twice, Stupid."

They stared at me.

"It means Nobody Anticipates The Storm."

They stared at me.

"It means Nothing Anchors The Ship."

My father frowned. Chopper woofed.

"It's STAN backward," Olivia said. "And how come you have a black eye? And where's Keith?"

"I'll explain later," I said to my father, cocking my head at Olivia. "Ix-nay on the Olive-ay?"

"How come you're cocking your head?" Olivia asked. "How come you're speaking pig latin?"

"Don't you think," I said, turning toward a broken display and beginning to clean up the glass, "that it's time for some little girls to get to work?"

Ten hours later, Olivia and Chopper piled back into the Fry-O-Lator. Olivia rolled down the window. "Aren't you coming, Stanny?"

"No, Peanut," I said, and then kissed her forehead. "But thank you *so* much. You and Chopper were a huge help. Really."

"Dad's taking us for ice cream," she said.

"I know."

"Real ice cream. Not frogurt."

"You earned it," I said. "Ask if they have Alpo frogurt for Chopper."

She laughed, a tinkly little sound as my father drove away. I walked to the pay phone in the center of town, fumbling for a quarter, and then took a deep breath. I dialed Ellen's house. Her mother answered on the second ring. The ice cubes were still there, firmly in cheek.

"Rigby residence?"

"Hi, um . . . this is Stan. Can I speak to Ellen, please?"

"I'm sorry, Stan, but Eleanor is not at home. Now, or at any time in the future. Permanently. Not home. Do you understand?"

"So I guess I can't leave a message, huh?"

"Correct."

I pulled out the yellow pages, leafing through the section under Lawyers. I dialed the first three numbers, busy, busy, voice mail. The third one, Blank, Wheaty, and Mumper, picked up on the first ring. I had an appointment in fifteen minutes.

The lobby of Blank, Wheaty, and Mumper was dark and not entirely clean. There were three offices and a small waiting room with one well-thumbed magazine, issue number forty-six of *American Quilter.* The secretary was a large woman with a large mole on her very large forehead.

"Take a seat."

I did, and watched the mole float up and down, like a coconut in the ocean, while she chewed gum and typed.

FIVE:

    1. List

    2. List

    3. List

    4. List

    5. List

Finally, she said, "Mrs. Mumper will see you now."

I walked down a short hallway and into a tiny office.

Going Nowhere

Behind a tiny desk and a tiny nameplate and a tiny stack of files, sat a very large Vanderlink, my old Assisted Learning teacher.

"Mrs. Vanderlink?"

"Actually," she said, "it's Vanderlink-Mumper now." She picked up the brass nameplate and looked wistfully at it. "They didn't have one big enough for the whole name. It's on order. Anyway, how can I help you?"

I sat down. "Don't you remember me, Mrs. Van . . . Vander . . . Mumper?"

She looked down at her wool business suit, removing some lint from the skirt. "No, I'm sorry, I don't."

"I'm Stan," I said. "Stan Smith? From Assisted Learning?"

She stopped pulling lint and looked up at me, recognition in her eyes. "Smith. Of course. The drawer of pictures."

Uh-oh.

"Sure," I said, "we used to draw a lot of pictures."

She frowned, sprinkling nonexistent lint on the floor. "Yes. Particularly ones of me tied to a tree, if I recall correctly. A rather buxom version of me. Full of arrows."

I laughed. A sad little laugh that died in my throat. "Yeah, sorry about that. I'm older now."

"I'm sure," she said. "At any rate, what can I do for you, Mr. Smith?"

I told her about Dos. And the need to make immediate bail, if only because of the food. And how, also, he was completely innocent, and how she needed to win the case for him. Like, right away.

"Well, we'll see. Bail we can do immediately."

"Thanks, Mrs. . . . Van . . . Va . . . Mump . . ."

"Think nothing of it, Smith. I will call you when the amount is set. You may now leave my office."

I walked to the park and sat on the bench. The ducks were still there. The bread crumbs were still there. I sat in the sun and absorbed feelings of martyrdom, which floated down in long yellow waves. If they wanted to come get me, they could get me. Whoever it was. The Barbie-doll leaver, the mystery tire slasher, the muscle car run-overer. I was too tired to care anymore. Bring 'em on. Besides, the ducks would protect me. "Right, guys?" I asked, causing the few ducks at my feet to go screeching off in fear.

Just as I was about to leave, full to the brim with self-pity, someone tapped my shoulder.

"Gaaah!" I said, which even ol' ponytail Steve Seagal will tell you is not a really cool or tough thing to say, and then jumped about three feet sideways.

"Whoa. You okay?"

It was Ellen Rigby. Yes, *that* Ellen Rigby.

"No, I'm not."

"Your mom said you might be here."

"She was right."

Ellen was wearing a ripped T-shirt and a Catholic schoolgirl/rocker skirt. Her shirt said BEEYATCH in red letters.

"I overheard what my mother said. So I called your house, and your mom answered. She was real helpful."

Going Nowhere

"That's my mom all right."

"You have a black eye," she said.

"So?"

Ellen shrugged. "And a swollen wrist. And cut elbows. You're not one of those *After School Special* kids who purposely hurt themselves, are you, Stan?"

FIVE WAYS I WAS GOING TO HURT MYSELF IF SO INCLINED:

1. Repeatedly poked in ribs with comfy pillow
2. Shoulders rubbed with aloe until painfully relaxed
3. Forced to endure untold hours of *Scantily Attired Nurse* footage
4. Feet held under lukewarm water until overly wrinkled
5. Subjected to Hungarian "Purring Kitten" torture

I frowned, gently touching the swelling around my eye. Why should I pretend? Why sit here and make small talk? I leaned forward.

"So why in hell did you kiss Miles? And why in the hell did you even go out with me?"

"It's like that, huh?" Ellen shrugged and then sat down. "Hell if I know, Stan."

"How can you not *know*? It's not a vocabulary quiz."

"That's true, Stan, and if boy geniuses could treat the whole world like a vocabulary quiz, they wouldn't have such a hard time living in it, would they?"

She had a point there. I didn't say anything.

Ellen shook her head and took a deep breath. "I dunno . . . it's like you had an idea of who I was in your mind, you know? I could see it written on your forehead, the panting and staring every time I came into Unhappy Video."

I pictured myself, at the counter. Yup, there I was, panting. Loser. I wondered why we deluded ourselves that we weren't being obvious when we were being *so* obvious. It's like when you recognize someone walking down the street but pretend you don't. And they recognize you and pretend *they* don't. And then you both just keep on walking.

"So, after a while, I decided since you like movies so much, I could play a role for you. Rita Hayworth in *Little Prissy Out on a Date*."

"So you did go out with Chad Chilton?"

She blushed a little. I had the feeling it was all she was capable of, a barely reddish spot about the size of a dime on her cheek.

"Not for very long."

"But why bother? Why pretend? And why me?"

Ellen played a drumroll on her thigh, faster and faster and finally spread her hands, palms up. "For an egghead you sure are stupid. I like Miles. It isn't obvious by now?"

It was obvious. It was so obvious it was ridiculous.

"I've liked him for a long time. But there was always

Cari. And he just kept ignoring me. And then there was you, looking at me with those hungry-dog eyes."

I scuffed my shoe in the dirt. There were spelt chunks arrayed in the grass, uneaten, that I could swear spelled out CHUMP.

"You still lied to me."

Ellen wiped some lipstick from her front teeth with her pinkie. "You ever lied to anyone, Stan?"

Hmmm. Tough to argue there. I shrugged. "Well, Miles is free now. You should call him up. Single and willing."

"No, sir," she said, faking a hillbilly accent for no reason I could tell. "I done changed my mind on that one."

"Why?"

"He's a lousy kisser."

I actually smiled. It was pretty funny.

"Quick!" she said. "Movies about relationships that don't work out!"

My brain automatically shuffled down an enormous group of titles, and I nearly began, in a dull monotone, a list that started with *Annie Hall.* Then I caught myself and said *"Fatal Attraction"* instead.

"Clever boy." She nodded. "As always."

"At least it's not a role. Good or bad, it's just me. Stan."

"Listen," she said, touching my arm. I drew away, but it wasn't easy. It still felt good to be touched. "Listen, I know what I did was kinda crappy. I'm sorry."

I felt like VanderMumper. Ellen had drawn some knockers on me and shot me full of arrows.

"But you play saxophone," I said lamely. "And you like good movies."

"So?"

She was right. Why had I thought that meant something? Idi Amin probably played saxophone. Charlie Manson liked good movies.

"I guess I thought it made you . . . different."

"Different than what?"

I didn't know what to say, and I'd forgotten to take my *Mentasis Futilis* pills, so I came up with this gem: "You didn't by any chance rob Happy Video the other night, did you?"

Ellen got up. "Have a good life, Stan."

"How about dolls?" I called. "You own any red dolls?"

She turned and walked away, after a while disappearing among the trees. It was just me and the ducks. When they flew out to the center of the pond, all together after some mysterious silent signal, it was just me.

I dragged my bike back over to the pay phone. It made a loud scraping noise the entire way and left white marks on the pavement. The pack of kids on their BMXs were still there, a miniature tough-guy gang with their sneers and their perfect tires.

"Ha-ha! Nice ride!" one said.

"What a dumb bike," the other said.

I nodded, letting my bike fall on its side with a crash. "You're right. It is a dumb bike."

They looked at one another, amazed. And then at me, in

unison, amazed. It was probably the first time anyone had ever told them "You're right." About anything. The sneers vanished.

"You sure spend a lot of time on the phone, mister."

"It's important," I answered.

"It's important," one kid told the others. "Give the man some room." They all backed up, saying stuff like "Give him some air," waiting for something to happen, maybe for someone to give birth or a bomb to explode. Everyone in the world had seen *way* too many movies. Of course, nothing did happen except my dialing. Eventually, the leader shrugged, and they all rode away in a pack.

The phone rang four times before Miles answered.

"Yo."

"That's how you answer the phone?" I asked. "What if the president's calling?"

"The president is *way* cooler than you think," Miles answered, without missing a beat. "He'd be like *'Whassup, dog?'*"

Neither of us said anything, fifteen seconds of silence during which the fight officially came to an end. I suddenly realized it was time to go, clear and clean and obvious. Leave. Split. Jump. Run. It was time to *become*. I was a bird. I was a bird that tweeted all the time about hating this nest but never having enough giblets to just get up and fly away. To see what happens when you're alone and no one's handing you free worms anymore.

I cleared my throat. "You wanna know something?"

"What?"

"We're going."

"Where?"

"California. You ready?"

"Are you serious?" Miles said, laughing. The way his voice wavered I could tell he was jumping up and down. "You better be serious, Jet Li, or I'm gonna come over there and punch you."

"You better bring an extra three people," I said. "I only showed you half my moves the other day."

"Awesome. *Such* the right decision."

"Start packing," I said. "Now."

"Right," he said, and hung up.

I rattled the change in my pocket as a cruiser pulled alongside me, Officer Dave in the driver's seat. He lowered the tinted window and then lowered his mirrored shades.

"Vandalizing public phones is a crime."

He looked even smaller and skinnier in the cruiser, with his seat belt and shorts and kneesocks.

"If by vandalizing you mean putting in way too many quarters for a lousy three-minute conversation, I am absolutely and completely guilty."

Officer Dave grinned like a shark. "Nice one." He put three sticks of gum into his mouth and chewed them angrily. "That stolen?"

I looked down at my bike. He looked down at my bike.

"Yeah," I said. "It is. While I was in the bike store at about midnight last night, I considered taking something shiny and expensive, but in the end this one just called to me."

Officer Dave blew a big bubble, which popped loudly.

Going Nowhere

Sweat glistened in his crewcut. "I know about you," he said. "The smart kid."

"You do?"

"All you smart kids."

"You mean smart like *smart-ass,* or smart like *beat up three times per chess-trophy*?"

Officer Dave revved the engine. The car bucked forward half a foot, and then stalled. He started it again with a roar. I wanted to tell him I knew about him, too. The kid that got picked on in school. A lot. The kid who got a badge and some sunglasses and a gun but hadn't changed a bit.

"So you want me to hit the siren?" he asked, approximating the noise in his throat. *"Wheer wheer."*

"No," I said.

He looked confused. "Kids usually like it when I hit the siren."

"I'm seventeen," I said.

He wasn't convinced. "So?"

I started to walk away, pulling the bike along with me.

"Looks like you could use a ride," Officer Dave called.

For once he was right. I was tired. And it was a long way back to my parents' house. "Can I have a ride?" I asked.

"Nope," he said, raising his window before pulling away. "Police policy."

I carried the bike on my shoulder half the way and dragged it the rest. By the time I got home, dinner (grilled formed vegetable protein with hearty cauliflower sauce) was on the table and my mother was annoyed I was late.

"Sit down, Stan," my father said.

"Hey, Stanny," Olivia said, sitting in the chair my father had invented for her. It was a big fluffy spider seat on a lever that moved her up or down and was controlled by a foot-pedal under my mother's chair. Smith's Toddler Tuffet. It was a prototype.

"Hi, Big O," I said, and kissed her forehead. Then I wiped some formed protein off her chin.

"So let's talk about Berkeley," my mother said, before my butt was even in its seat.

"So let's not."

My father sighed, helping himself to a big ladleful of mush.

"I've got too much on my plate right now as it is," I said, mostly meaning the huge mound of formed protein, but also the fact that someone was stalking me. "Someone is stalking me."

"And this stalker," my mother asked, "this is the person who has given you the bruises and destroyed Happy Video and is the reason behind all your strange behavior?"

"Yes," I said.

"We had Alpo frogurt," Olivia said, the tuffet leaning to one side.

"Stan did a terrific job putting that store back in order," my father said, too quickly, hoping to avoid the subject of real ice cream. "A lot of hard work."

"Terrific," my mother said. "So no college, but a great future in carpentry."

Going Nowhere

"Script writing," I said.

Chopper groaned and lifted his leg.

"Don't even think about it," my mother warned, pointing.

Chopper put his leg back down. Then there was a long and silent dinner, one with no dessert and no resolution and no way to even begin explaining why it suddenly felt so right to go to California. With Miles. For no reason at all. With no money. Or job. Or a big comfy, slightly leaning bed to hide in for a week. Either way, I needed to tell my parents. I opened my mouth, but just couldn't make my brain kick in. My tongue started to get dry and my jaw started to hurt, but no sound came out. Olivia looked at me. My father looked at me. I pictured myself standing on a chair in a safari outfit, cracking a whip at my growling brain while trying to make it jump through a hoop. It reared up and bit my calf instead. My mother reached for the ladle, spooning out seconds.

After my parents had gone up to their room, I snuck back downstairs and made a long-distance call.

"Hello?"

"Uncle Stu? This is Stan?"

"Hello? What? Who?"

"Stan? Your nephew? Calling from Millville?"

"Of course," he said, even though it was obvious he had no idea who I was. "My favorite nephew. Stan."

"Listen, Uncle Stu, I wanted to ask you a question about your script."

"Who is this?" Uncle Stu snapped. "DJ Forty-Foot Burrito's lawyer? Listen, the lawsuit is over, okay? You lost. This is harassment! You want a harassment charge now, too?"

"Uncle Stu, this really is *Stan,*" I said. "Your sister's son? I'm calling because I'm thinking of writing my own script. Or maybe not. To be honest, I can't decide. And also I have no ideas. But I need to figure if I'm wasting my time, you know? And so I thought maybe you could help. Like, let me know if it's worth it. Or how to start. And finish. And the middle too, you know what I mean?"

"Harassment," Uncle Stu said. A noise got louder in the background. It sounded like the motor for a hot tub. "You want another taste of my lawyer? Just keep it up."

The line went dead. Somewhere in the house Chopper sighed, a wheeze that was like letting the entire world slide off your shoulders all at once.

CHAPTER EIGHTEEN

THE FAST *actually really not all that fast...maybe even a tad slow* **AND THE** *actually not all that furious...maybe even sort of pleased* **FURIOUS**

In the morning, I dragged my bike to Keith's house. It was heavy and my shoulders were sore and my neck and wrist and back and ankles hurt. A couple of times I thought I heard a big muscle car coming and ducked into the bushes, but both times it was just Chevettes with lousy mufflers.

FIVE THINGS ONE TYPICALLY LEARNS WHILE
SPENDING TOO MUCH TIME IN THE BUSHES:
1. Dirt is cold and wet.
2. Bugs live in there, but prefer your neck.
3. When a raccoon is surprised and hisses and then rears back on its hind legs, it is almost never a good idea to continue forward under a bush and say things like "Nice raccoon. Pretty raccoon."
4. If you got lost in the woods and were forced to live off what you could forage

amongst the bushes, you'd try approximately one nibble of mossy bark and then just lie down and starve.

5. Emerging from the bushes just when that really short woman who works at the drugstore comes jogging by in her teal sweatsuit and scaring her and then watching confusedly as she screams and tries to climb a tree and then brushing mud off your face so she recognizes you and then helping her back down the six inches she made it up the trunk and apologizing profusely is pretty much a lousy idea.

I'd never been to Keith's house before, which was actually an apartment in an L-shaped building over a cement courtyard with blooms of flowers and animal-shaped shrubbery. Very un-Keith. I leaned my bike against the mailboxes without locking it, then taped a note on the crossbar. It said: "TRY SLASHING THE TIRES NOW, JACKOFF. YOU WANNA STEAL THE WHOLE THING? GO AHEAD."

I rang Keith's bell. There was no answer, so I rang it six times. I rang it one time for six minutes. I rang it to the rhythm of "Super Freak," by Rick James. Finally there was an annoyed voice.

"What?"

"Keith, it's me," I said. "Stan. Let me in."

Going Nowhere

"I don't know any Stan," the voice said, and then shut off the microphone. I hit the buzzer nine more times. Then I gave up and climbed the fence. The wires sticking out at the top were pointy and cut my hand. It was becoming a collection. When I got to Keith's door, I kicked it, three times, hard. While I was winding for the fourth, he opened up. It was too late to stop my leg, so I kicked him in the shin.

"Ouch," he said. He was wearing an orange bathrobe that was ratty and stained, and smiley-face boxers. His enormous belly jutted out, covered with hair. His legs were pale and white, except the shin, where I'd kicked it, which was red and would soon be blue. He needed a shave and a haircut and a mustache trim. In one hand he held an enormous bag of M&M's, the size of a pillowcase.

"You need a mustache trim," I said.

Keith shrugged, and left the door open, walking back into the apartment. It was clean and neat and tastefully decorated. There were chintz curtains and framed Klimt prints and matching lamps. It was completely impossible.

"No way," I said.

"Way," he said. I followed him as he flopped onto the couch. The springs groaned. He pulled a blanket over himself and looked at the ceiling. "What you want?"

I found the remote and turned down the volume of the sports channel. An announcer was screaming about the lack of foresight in one team calling a time-out with six seconds left, when they should really have waited until there were only five seconds left. It gave me pleasure to cut him off.

"I want you to come with me."

Keith groaned. "Where?"

"It's a surprise."

"Do they serve beer at the surprise?"

"No."

"Do they have Supreme Nachos at the surprise?"

"No."

"Then I'm not going."

"Yes, you are," I said. I grabbed his arm and tried to pull him up. He didn't budge. I grabbed his leg and yanked and tugged. He didn't move an inch. He reached for a handful of M&M's and started humming. I went into the kitchen and found a broom. I jammed it between the cushion and his back, and with a mighty shove, levered him onto the floor. He landed facedown, nose mashed into the carpet, and just lay there, motionless. His breath stirred dust bunnies that raced under a desk.

"C'mon, Keith," I said. "Get up!"

"Why bother?" he said. "My store is ruined. The delinquents have finally taken over. What's the point?"

"They haven't taken over," I said. "Really. I can prove it. But you have to come with me."

"It's comfortable down here," he said.

I began to whack him with the broom. I started with his feet and worked upward. When I got to his shoulders, he stood and said, "All right already."

"Go get dressed," I told him. "And get your car keys. I'm driving."

Going Nowhere

* * * *

Outside, there was a new note on the crossbar of my bike. It said: YOOURE GONNNA GET ITS. GETS IT. GET IT. For a second it terrified me. After that, I was just plain scared.

"What's that mean?" Keith asked.

"Nothing." I put the bike in the trunk of his massive Lincoln. Inside, I adjusted the seat forward and then pulled a pair of his boxers out of my pocket. I'd found them in his dresser. They had little blue lambs all over them.

"Those are my boxers," he said.

"This is your blindfold," I corrected, and pulled them over his head.

"I can't see."

"That's the point," I said, and then peeled out into the street.

"You're driving too fast," he said.

"How do you know? You're blind."

"I can smell it."

"That's not driving too fast you smell," I said.

Keith shrugged and then began forcing potato chips through the fly.

We pulled behind the store, crunching slowly over gravel until we were a few feet from the back door.

"Are there doctors at the surprise? I don't like doctors."

"No doctors," I said, taking Keith's hand and leading him into Happy Video. I turned on the lights and arranged him in the center of the room.

"Okay, you can take your boxers off."

Keith reached down and started unbuckling his belt.

"The other boxers," I said.

"Oh." He pulled the lambs off his face, freeing his mustache and eyes and afro. Happy Video was completely cleaned up. The holes in the walls were fixed and the whole thing was repainted a pleasing yellow. There were new pine shelves along one wall, my father having figured out a way of building them so they had twice the display room of the old shelves. And they only leaned a little to the left. There were new cubicles in the center to display *New Arrivals*. There was an expanded *Classics* section. There was a display case my father had built for cameras and VCRs and DVD players, with a sliding glass door that actually slid. In the wrong direction, but it still slid. There were new posters and bunting that Olivia had picked out and strung. There was even a porno room, with a swinging saloon door, like in a John Wayne movie, instead of the old curtain. The place smelled a little farty, but even that felt right, a loving contribution from Chopper.

"Wow," Keith said. The place looked great. It looked fantastic. "Wow," he said again.

"Well?" I said. "What do you want to do?"

He wiped a tear from his eye. He ran his big hands over the new cabinet, and then along his new desk.

"Open up, I guess," he finally said.

I went to the front of the store and tore down the yellow police tape. I propped the door open and turned the CLOSED sign around. I looked back at Keith, who was still in awe. By the time I got to the desk, one of the BMX kids had stuck his head in and said, "Hey, guy, you got *The Terminator*?"

I worked most of a shift, and when it was over accepted a hug from Keith.

FIVE THINGS MORE DESIRABLE THAN KEITH-HUG:
1. Lowered into oatmeal vat
2. Forced to wear Timmy the Sock Puppet costume
3. Hugged by reasonably hygienic Sasquatch
4. In the center of a week-long group sneeze
5. Being the favorite soft thing in the pocket of Lennie from *Of Mice and Men.*

"You, Stan, have both impressed and surprised me."

I said "Mmmpfhneff" for a while, until Keith let go, and then I said, "thanks."

Outside, my bike was gone. Completely. Just not there. No notes or further damage. Gone. Actually, it was a relief. My shoulder already felt better. By the time I'd walked home, what with having to dive into the bushes fifteen times (fourteen Chevettes and a Corolla), it was getting dark. Miles was in the driveway, leaning on his car.

"You, Stan, are covered with dirt and leaves."

"I just applied for a job as a tree," I said. It made so little sense, he didn't even bother responding.

"Anyway, I think we have a problem."

"What?"

"My car's acting weird. I think there's really something wrong. I'm not sure we're going for Slurpees, let alone to Cali."

He leaned over the hood and pointed to a bunch of stuff: tubes, valves, metal parts.

"Maybe it's that tube," I pointed.

"It's not that tube."

"Maybe it's that valve."

"It's not that valve."

"Maybe my dad could check it out."

Miles looked askance. He peered back at his engine protectively. "I dunno. You sure I let him get his hands on it, it's not gonna suddenly run on Pop-Tarts?"

"Shut up," I said.

We walked into the backyard. My father was at his worktable, lowering rusted gears into a bucket of some solution. We peered over, watching the grease and rust flaking away.

"New thing I'm working on. Smith's E-Z Instant Cleaner."

"Looks like it works pretty good," Miles said.

My father stroked his beard. "Unfortunately a bit too good." He pointed to the bucket, where the gear was now completely shiny, almost new in parts, and then to other buckets where the gears themselves had begun to dissolve. My father went to the chalkboard and erased part of an equation, then wrote in a missing cosine. Then he added a four and an NaCl.

Going Nowhere

"Dad? Miles is having some problems with his car. Can you look at it?"

"Are you going to tell me the truth if I ask why Miles has a swollen nose?"

"Definitely," Miles said.

"Not," I said.

"Fine," my father said. "How about your eye? Or wrist? Or neck? Is this a NATS thing?"

"No," I said.

"NATS?" Miles asked.

"I was busy hating you then," I said. "I'll tell you later."

"Chad Chilton?" Miles guessed.

"Who?" my father asked.

"Can we PLEASE go look at the car?"

My father scratched behind his ear with the tip of a plumb bob. "How about we go see this car?"

"Good idea," Miles agreed.

We walked out to the driveway, Chopper following behind and panting heavily from the thirty-yard exertion.

"Miles and I are going to California," I said. "Instead of college. Or whatever."

My father blinked. He looked at his feet and his hands. "Really?"

"Yes."

"And I assume, since the house is not on fire, you haven't told your mother yet?"

I nodded. "Correct."

Faster

When we reached the car, my father sighed. "You intend to go in this?"

"The MilesMobile," Miles said proudly.

My father peered under the hood. Then pulled out about three feet of worn rubber tubing. "Not if you want to make it over the county line."

"I told you it was that tube," I said.

"That's not the tube you pointed to," Miles said.

My father then pulled out a little metal box that looked like a fan. It was a fan. "Bearings are shot here, too."

"We're screwed," I said.

"We're screwed," Miles said.

"Well, I have a surprise for you." My father smiled. "I was saving it, but I suppose now is as good a time as any."

"Smith's E-Z Flying Carpet?" Miles guessed.

"Smith's E-Z Atomic Transporter?" I guessed.

My father led us into the garage. A round shape was hidden under three white tarps. He yanked them off, one at a time, as an orange VW bus was slowly revealed.

"Whoa!" said Miles.

"What's that?" I asked.

"Yours," my father said.

"Mine?"

"Yours."

"COOL!" Miles said. "OURS!"

He popped the rear door and checked out the engine. I checked out the big whale-fin spoiler on the roof. There was also a huge pair of metal antlers welded to the front, and a red button on the dashboard that said LIFT OFF beneath it.

"What's that do?" I asked.

"Never, ever touch that," my father said. "Ever."

I immediately pressed it. Nothing happened. He smiled.

"Dad, you *do* have a sense of humor."

"Shhh," he said. "Don't tell your mother."

Miles climbed off the luggage rack and slapped my father five. "What a ride! Way to go, Mr. S!"

"But what does it run on?" I asked.

My father smiled. "What do you think? Vegetable oil."

He was so proud, I couldn't act disappointed. But I didn't have to when I looked at Miles and he was beaming. "Vegetable oil! Awesome! Those hippie California chicks *love* the environment!"

Miles threw the door open and climbed inside. There was red carpet in the back and posters on the sides and a tiny fridge and a little desk and tools and bunks on the walls that folded in when you weren't sleeping. It was unbelievable.

"It's the van I always wanted when I was in college," my father said.

"Mr. S, this so *rules*!" Miles said.

"Is this what you've been working on all this time?" I asked. "This must have taken forever."

My father shrugged.

"But what about your other inventions? And where did you get the money?"

"Well, actually, I sold my plans for bio-diesel conversion to GM twenty years ago. As it turns out, we're pretty well-off."

"But — but . . . ," I stammered.

"You're a rich kid?" Miles laughed. "You need a new haircut, Trump Jr."

"Your mother and I wanted you to work for what you have. To understand that things aren't always given to you. The money is tied up in investments. In the meantime, we were determined to live a normal life."

"Normal?" I said.

"Normal?" Miles said.

"Well, I suppose you could make an argument either way," my father admitted.

"What about the store?" I asked.

"Your mother enjoys the store, but I don't think we've made a cent since it opened."

"Finally, something I already knew."

He laughed. "But that's between you and me."

I slapped myself on the forehead. "Then I need to borrow some cash, Dad, like, right now!"

He reached into his back pocket for the wallet he'd invented, Smith's Secure-a-Let. He struggled for a while, unable to get it open.

"Let me try," Miles said, squeezing and pulling. He couldn't open it, either.

"What do you need money for, anyway?"

"Dos's bail."

My father nodded. "A very odd Mumper woman called this afternoon. It's already taken care of. Dos is at his house right now, I believe."

"Well, then," I said, amazed that things seemed to be actually, kinda, sorta working out, "let's go see him."

CHAPTER NINETEEN
THE *fourth, fifth, sixth, and* SEVENTH *blubbery* SEAL

Miles and I walked across the field.

"Your dad is so frickin' cool, you know that?"

"I guess I do now," I said. Why hadn't I noticed before?

Miles felt his cheekbone with two fingers. "Does my bruise look like it's healed any?"

"I can bring it back for you," I said, cocking a fist.

He laughed. "I'll pass."

"What were we fighting about again?" I asked.

"I dunno? Some girl or something? Or maybe it was just bad kielbasa."

"That's right," I said, and slapped my forehead. "Never trust German food."

We got to Dos's front steps, and had a hard time staying on them as they were slanted to the right.

"Cool as your dad is, he isn't very level."

"I know," I said. "I think it's an inner ear problem. I think it's genetic."

Going Nowhere

Miles almost fell off the step. I grabbed his shoulder as Dos opened the door.

"Amigo!" I said.

"Dos!" Miles said.

Dos didn't say a word. Kids ran around behind him, playing some sort of game with a ball and sticks and pillows, screaming in Spanish. Mrs. Dos stood in the hallway, beaming. Dos got me in a bear hug and then pulled us into the house.

"Ohmygod, I'm stuffed," Miles said, holding his stomach as we walked back across the lettuce field. Mrs. Dos had made an enormous spread and I'd eaten enough steak to choke a cow.

"Tell me about it."

The stars were bright and the field smelled like fresh greens and it was a beautiful night. I pointed out Orion for Miles.

"The deer?" he guessed.

"No, the hunter."

He pointed to Pleiades. "Constellation Hendrix?"

"Nope," I said. "Good guess, though."

"What is it really?"

I was about to say the seven sisters, when I noticed something on the roof of Smith's Natural Foods. It sure wasn't a weather vane.

"Do you see that?"

Miles squinted. "You mean that extremely fat thing on the roof?"

"Exactly."

"Nope," he said. "Don't see it."

"Let's go check it out."

We circled around the side of the store and hunkered in a corn row.

"Why are we playing marines?" Miles whispered.

I didn't say anything.

"Why am I whispering?" Miles asked.

"I think it's Chad Chilton. He's probably painting dolls up there. We've got him dead to rights. *Finally* someone will believe me."

"We?" Miles said.

I signaled for him to follow and began flanking the building, coming around back, until we could pop out of a furrow and be at the side door.

"What are we going to do after we surprise him?" Miles asked. "Like, he's big and we're small. It's really not that surprising."

"No time for thinking," I said, palming his forehead. "It's time for action! It's time to channel Van Damme!"

"I hate Van Damme."

"How about Bruce Lee?"

"He's cool."

"Good, 'cause all this BS needs to end. Like, right now."

I ran out into the yard first, Miles behind me, but there was nothing on the roof. Had we been imagining it? Just another case of hallucinatory beef overload? Then I saw my bike. In the middle of the yard. Half-buried, with the other half stuck out of the ground, handlebars bent like sculpture. It looked like a deer. In pain. Plus, the whole thing was painted. Bright red.

"Ohmygod," I said, my body hot and cold at the same time.

"Really, really weird," Miles said. "Seriously twisted."

I wanted to run. It was so far past a joke. I needed ten eyes, to see in every direction instead of swiveling my head and panting. There was someone seriously and majorly bent. Like jail and injection bent. Jason in Millville. It was Wednesday the twelfth. Close enough. Miles and I squatted, looking around. Were we being watched? It was quiet, just crickets and the occasional bird, no movement or sound.

"You know what this is just like?"

"What?" I hissed.

"So Scooby-Doo."

"Shh . . . ," I said.

"Except there's no hot Velma," Miles whispered. "Or a cool crime-fighting van. Or a talking dog. Or snacks."

"Will you shut up?"

"I have to pee."

"Go ahead."

"Too late," Miles said, then grabbed my hand and stuck it in a puddle near his foot. I almost yelled, then saw it was just water.

"Got ya," he said.

The yard was still quiet. The cricket sounds were gone and the bird sounds were gone. Maybe we were just freaking each other out.

"Maybe we should go," I said.

"Good idea," Miles said, standing up.

"Hang on." I grabbed his arm. "Do you smell something?"

He sniffed. "Actually . . ."

I sniffed. "It smells like —"

Prarash ran out from behind an old tractor wheel and grabbed Miles from behind. We both screamed. Really and truly like little girls. It was almost funny, except it wasn't. Prarash was naked from the waist up, just a sheet wrapped around his midsection. He had a big red dot painted on his forehead and was covered with hair, like an ape. A fat ape. He glistened, even under the stars. He also smelled like very, very old beer. It was a smell I could not mistake. It smelled like Keith after his worst night, times a thousand. Times twenty thousand.

"*You're* the one, Fred?" I said, in disbelief. "You're the one with the tires and the car and the notes?"

Prarash gripped Miles tighter. "What did you call me?"

"Umm . . . sorry," I said. "Prarash."

His grip relaxed a little, but not enough for Miles to pull away. Prarash held him against his sheet.

"But you don't even *own* a car," I said stupidly. "Cars are bad for the ozone."

"What is owning?" he snarled. "None of us owns anything."

"Okay . . . but why were you on the roof? And what's with the dolls?"

"What's with the dolls?" he mimicked, in a baby voice.

"You want a beer, dude?" Miles offered. "Just let go of me and I'll grab you one from the car."

Prarash yanked his hair, and Miles cried out. I heard a bark. It could have been any dog, really. But then I heard a fart and there was no mistaking it.

"Chopper?" I said.

"Scooby?" Miles guessed.

"Stanny?" came a small voice, from inside the store.

"Olivia?"

"Don't move," Prarash said. Miles cried out.

"I swear," I said, trying to feel tough, but on the verge of tears. "I swear, if you *hurt* her?"

"The question the young bee should be asking itself," Prarash said, "is what you're going to do when I hurt *you.*"

Prarash hit Miles on the back of the head. Miles made an "oof" sound and fell to the grass. Then Prarash walked toward me. "Your sister and I and the disgusting animal took a walk because everyone knows wherever Olivia goes, the young bee is sure to follow."

I backed toward the door. Chopper was barking loudly now, working himself into a frenzy.

"What is it you want? What is your problem?"

"My problem?" Prarash sneered. "You, Stan-lee, have *always* been my problem."

It was like a German movie that had started weird and had just gotten weirder. People dancing in black turtlenecks and close-ups of earlobes and Adam's apples. This was now officially

Faster

a video you'd pull out of your VCR and toss on the lawn. I reached around on the ground for a weapon, for anything, and came up with a petrified yam. Prarash laughed, his eyes wide, the size of manholes. "The young bee is all out of options."

I threw the yam, missing badly. He didn't bother to duck, and swung in a wide arc. I did bother to duck, and his big, fat, dangerous (who knew) hippie fist slammed into a plank behind me. I circled left, as he moved in again. I clenched my fists, back pressed against a tomato bin. There was no room to slide, either right or left. Olivia yelled again. I cocked my arm, trying to re-member the improbable way I'd connected with Miles's nose.

"Wait!" I said.

"Wait?" he said.

"Wait," my mother said, and then strode into the circle of moonlight and decked Prarash with a right cross so powerful three teeth went flying into the air, fluttering for a second like moths, before falling to the dirt. Prarash made a slobbery sound before collapsing like a sock full of pudding.

"Wow, Mom," I said.

She adjusted her big hoop earrings and smoothed her skirt, looking down at Prarash in a heap at her feet. "Wow, yourself." She blew on her knuckles and shook her hand up and down like a rag. "Funny how much that hurts."

I stood there in awe. My mother the hero. Joan of Bark. The Vegan Avenger. Muhammad Yam-li.

Miles stood wobbily and walked over, rubbing his scalp like it was just another day. "Hey there, Mrs. S."

Going Nowhere

My mother pulled at the lock of Smith's Natural Foods. "Well, don't just stand there, young man. Run over to Roberto's and call Sheriff Conner while I let your sister out of the store."

Sheriff Conner drove up twenty minutes later, lights flashing as the cruiser bounced across my mother's arugula patch. I held Olivia in my arms while Miles fed her little pieces of beef jerky every time my mother turned her head. Olivia was remarkably relaxed, like she was locked into a yam hut by crazy fat yogis three days a week.

"Stan! Hi, buddy!"

"Hi, Sheriff."

Sheriff Conner cinched his belt and pushed up his hat with the tip of his shotgun. "So what exactly is going on here?"

I pointed with my foot at Prarash. "Completely excellent question."

Sheriff Conner crouched over, examining Fred. "Whoa, Mrs. Smith, that's quite a knotting-up you've done here."

Prarash rolled in the mud. My mother had roped him like a calf. He rolled to say something, but it mostly sounded like "Mmmmffrreeempfh," since my mother had also shoved a rotted lettuce head into his mouth.

Sheriff Conner looked in Prarash's face. "Now, why don't you calm down so I can loosen this rig and get you in a nice pair of handcuffs, huh? Or are we gonna have to do this the hard way?"

Prarash stopped struggling and Sheriff Conner yanked the lettuce head from his teeth.

"Has it come to this, Sirena?" Prarash cried, spitting lettuce juice. "Are you ready to forsake me?"

We all looked at one another. Sirena?

"Who's that?" I asked.

"I think he's been smoking that lettuce, too," Miles said.

"No," my mother said, blushing. "I'm afraid that's me."

"What?"

"Little dove, now is the time to prove yourself! Do you not remember our walks down the paths of Veda? Our strolls through fields of Chi and Longing?"

"Mom?" I said. "This is getting weird."

"Getting?" Miles said.

"He smells," Olivia said.

Chopper picked up the cue, raised his leg, and peed on Prarash's neck.

"Sorry, Sheriff," my mother apologized.

"No problemo," Sheriff Conner said. "I believe that's the closest thing to a shower this character's had in months."

My mother sighed. "I've known for some time that Frederick here had developed some . . . feelings for me. I just didn't realize to what extent."

"But the dolls? And the flats? And a *nickname*?"

"YOU!" Prarash yelled, his eyes crazy, staring at me. "You were poisoning me to her! Always with your smart comments and your little jokes."

My father walked up and shined the flashlight he'd invented in Prarash's face, Smith's E-Z Beam. Prarash didn't even squint. It wasn't very bright. In fact, it may not have made any light at all. My father took my mother's hand. "It finally happened, huh?"

My mother nodded.

My father scratched his head. "I know I promised the day we were married I'd never say 'I told you so,' but . . ."

"Keep the streak alive," my mother suggested.

Sheriff Conner got Prarash unknotted and on his feet and into a pair of cuffs. Fred began to weep. I couldn't believe it, but I actually felt a little bad for him. He pointed at me with his runny nose. "Why wouldn't you just *go away*? Could you not see what your mother and I were about to *share*?"

"Hoo boy," my father said.

"Hoo boy," my mother said.

Maybe Prarash was right. Maybe *that's* why I'd stayed around. Why I'd gotten bad grades and hadn't applied to colleges. Maybe subconsciously I'd known all along this would happen. And I'd be needed.

I turned toward my parents. "You know what? Maybe subconsciously . . ."

"Forget it," my mother said.

"No one's buying it," my father said.

"Nice try, though," Miles said.

"I am leaving, though," I told Prarash. It felt good to say. Better every time. "I'm going to California."

My mother raised an eyebrow. "What?"

Olivia raised an eyebrow. "What?"

Prarash wiped his beard on his shoulder and moaned. "I've always had lousy timing."

Faster

Sheriff Conner shoved Prarash into the backseat, not delivering the usual speech about "watch your head," and Prarash slammed into the back with a crunch. Sheriff Conner got in the front and then leaned out the window. "Give my apologies to Roberto. Just part of the job, you know."

The cruiser sped away with the lights flashing, tearing another trail through the arugula.

"So much for this year's harvest," my mother said.

"There's always next year," my father consoled. "That's the amazing thing about nature. Stuff just keeps growing."

Olivia had fallen asleep in my arms. My father took her and began walking back to the house. Chopper trotted behind, licking at her dangling fingers. Miles gave a salute and said he was going to go home and sleep for about ten years. When we were alone, I looked at my mother.

"You were *about* to make him leave? Why did you even let it go this long?"

My mother stared at her feet. "I've been trying to think of a way to let Frederick know he needed to move on for quite some time, but I guess I got lulled into overlooking some things."

"What things?"

"Just about all of them." She sighed. "Mostly, I suppose, I let it go because he's the only one who ever really listens to me."

I took her by the hand and we started walking back toward the house. "You know something, Mom? If there is one single thing in the world I absolutely and completely understand, that's definitely it."

"Well, that's good, I suppose."

Going Nowhere

We stepped over a row of zucchini together.

"So, I'm going to California with Miles next week."

"Yes, I heard."

"And?"

She held up my hand and kissed it and sighed. "Be careful driving."

I laughed. "You know, I guess I could check Berkeley out when I get there. No promises, but, since I'll be there anyway . . ."

"Okay, Stanley," she said.

And it was. Okay.

CHAPTER TWENTY

A **RESERVOIR** *of nostalgia for a town about to be left to the* **DOGS**

My parents held a going-away party for Miles and me behind Smith's Natural, which was now closed. Permanently. My mother made a huge pot of organic chili that no one went anywhere near, mostly because it smelled almost exactly like a combination of old socks and slightly newer socks. There were picnic tables and a barbecue pit and horseshoes and a radio playing mariachi music. Mrs. Dos and Mrs. Tres were cooking an enormous spread, tamales, roast pork, flautas, ceviche, *pollo asado,* and huge plates of chilies and avocado. Their kids tore around, screaming at one another in Spanish. My father stood under an almond tree drinking a beer (drinking a beer?). My mother stirred her chili and talked with Mrs. Uno about turning Smith's Natural into a taqueria.

I walked across the lettuce patch, smiling at Olivia and Dos's son, who were holding hands on the spot where I'd dug up and then fully buried my poor bike. We'd had a little ceremony for it. Miles had read a few words (Nirvana lyrics) and then

Going Nowhere

Olivia had rung a handlebar bell twenty-one times. Next to her, Keith was eating slices of a big white frosted cake he'd brought himself. He had a slice in each hand and was alternating between them.

"Yeah, they arrested the bastard," he said, mustache covered in frosting. Then he looked down at Olivia. "Sorry, honey."

"It's okay," she said. "I know what it means. I know *who* it means, too."

"Quién?" said Dos's son. "Who?"

"I'll tell you later," Olivia said.

"They found traces of organic dirt in our carpet. Found it all over his tent, too," Keith explained.

"Yurt," Olivia said.

"When they raided the tent, they found some pretty interesting stuff. Like, for instance, the entire Happy Video porno collection." Keith looked at Olivia again and covered her ears. "Sorry, honey."

"S'okay," she said. "Yurt."

"They also found a bunch of spray-painted dolls." Keith took a huge bite of cake. Then he said "Weird, huh?" except his mouth was so full of food, it sounded like "Mrouweref, Fnurt?"

"What about my shift?" I asked. "Have you found someone to cover it?"

Keith smiled. "Yeah, Officer Dave is going to take over."

"Officer Dave?" I said. "No way."

"Way," Keith said, finishing both his slices and then

picking up two more. "Turns out he hates being a cop. He's a movie buff. Big Arnold fan. He quit the force a week ago. Starts training Monday."

"Is he doing the books now, too?"

Keith frowned, licking his fingers. "Doing the books is my job, Stan."

"Yeah, of course," I said.

"Hey, Stan!" Keith yelled. "Stallone movies!"

"No," I said, shaking my head. "Not today."

"C'mon!" he yelled again, getting excited. "One last time! Check this out, everybody! Reverse alphabetical!"

I sighed and began a monotone, *"Victory. Tango & Cash. Staying Alive. Rocky V. Rocky IV . . ."*

"Well, hell-o," I heard my mother saying. She was shaking hands with Dr. Felder. When she turned, he winced, looking down at his red fingers. I walked over to where he stood under an almond tree, sipping from a Dixie cup of milk. He wore khaki shorts and a yellow sweater tied around his shoulders.

"Hey, Doc," I said. "Sporty outfit."

He looked down, as if surprised to see himself wearing sandals, then wiggled his toes.

"I got a gift certificate," he explained. "For Christmas."

"Christmas was a long time ago," I said.

"Yeah," Dr. Felder agreed, sipping milk. "I guess I haven't had a lot of time for stuff like shopping."

"Too busy fixing the heads of upset teendom, huh?"

Dr. Felder smirked, but not much. "Listen, I thought a

lot about what you said in my office, Stan, and I'm sorry for questioning whether you might have broken into the store."

"To be honest, Doc? You should be."

He adjusted his sweater. "You're right. It's a bit embarrassing, actually. The thing is, I've been treating Prarash for years. I don't know how it could have taken this long to start connecting the dots. And then, when I finally did, I really should have called the police. Like, immediately."

"Wait a minute," I said, incredulous. "You *see* Prarash?"

Dr. Felder nodded. "Oh, yes. One of my most difficult patients. He needs quite a bit of help. Hopefully he'll get some in prison."

"Yeah," I said. "Hopefully, he'll get a whole lot of something in prison."

Olivia came tearing past us, followed by Dos's son. They ran laughing behind a pile of yams.

"So, in the meantime," Dr. Felder said, "I've decided to give up on therapy for a while."

"Give up?"

Dr. Felder looked pained. His face turned red and he seemed to be sweating. I'd never seen him sweat before.

"Well, maybe not so much give up. More like take a break."

I didn't say anything, allowing him to organize his thoughts.

"I guess this whole incident has made me realize I've been coloring by the numbers, you know? Taking things for granted. Mostly, not listening. I mean *really* listening."

"Kiss of death for a therapist," I said.

He laughed. "Don't I know it. So, actually, I'm going to Italy for a couple of months. See some art. And old buildings."

"Good for you, Doc," I said.

"Plus, I will be receiving my own treatment. From a renowned Italian psychotherapist."

"Wow," I said, impressed. "Time to check out the other end of the couch, huh?"

"Exactly."

He smiled and toasted me with his milk. I smiled and toasted him with my cherry Coke.

"Can I ask you one last thing?"

"Sure."

"What's your first name?"

Dr. Felder's smile went away. He looked off into the fields for a long time, finally nodding as if he'd come to terms with something.

"Boris."

"Boris?" I said, doing a spit-take with the Coke. "You're joking."

He shook his head, wiping cola off his shorts. "No, actually I'm not. It's been a source of . . . embarrassment for quite some time."

"Boris Felder," I said. "Man, that's almost worse than Stan Smith."

"It almost is," Boris agreed, and then walked over to the picnic table to freshen his milk.

* * * *

Going Nowhere

Toward the end of lunch, Miles stood up from his seat at the picnic table and announced in a voice two octaves below his normal one, "We Must Go Now."

Everyone shook their heads, knowing he was right, except Keith, who grabbed the taco platter and said, "I'm not finished."

"Sprout-water diet," I told him.

"No chance," he said, then picked up a beef taco and gave it a big kiss.

Miles backed the van up in front of the barn and we loaded the last of our stuff, mostly CDs and leftover food. Everyone gathered around, my father shaking Miles's hand, and then mine. He leaned over and kissed me on the forehead and handed me five hundred-dollar bills.

"Drive safe, okay?"

Keith got me a bear hug that smelled like cake and Keith, which was not the greatest combination, then handed me five one-dollar bills. "Go ahead and drive reckless. What can it hurt?"

My mother gave Miles directions to the highway.

"I know the way to the highway, Mrs. Smith," Miles said.

"I hope you find what you're looking for," she told me, then kissed me in the exact same spot my father had.

"Me, too," I said, then hugged Dos and Mrs. Dos and the kids. I thought there was a chance Olivia wouldn't cry, but that chance came and went.

"Can't I come?"

"Sorry, Peanut."

"Can't you not go?"

FIVE REASONS NOT TO GO:
1. Olivia
2. Olivia
3. Olivia
4. Olivia and Chopper
5. Olivia

"I'll be back soon," I said. "Then we can go and feed the ducks."

She sniffled and shook her head, and my mother took her by the hand and led her away. Chopper woofed and howled and peed on the tires. Miles and I climbed into the van and started up the driveway, everyone waving. At least until the van stalled. My father grabbed a wrench and ran toward us, but Miles got it restarted, with an enormous backfire, and we pulled past Smith's Soon to Be Natural Taqueria with a lurch, heading toward the highway.

"Wait, I'm lost," Miles said, pretending to turn the wheel. "Should we go back and ask directions?"

"Shut up," I said.

"Wait, I'm hungry," he said, pretending to turn the wheel in the opposite direction. "Should we go back for more tacos?"

Going Nowhere

"Just drive," I said.

"So we're going? Definitely?"

"Definitely," I said.

"Good." Miles nodded, almost running over the mailbox. "Just making sure."

CHAPTER TWENTY-ONE
OUT *not entirely* OF THE *very recent* PAST

We made it about half a mile past the YOU ARE NOW LEAVING MILL-VILLE, HAVE A GOOD TRIP! sign, when a red light went on in the dashboard. Miles flicked it a couple of times with his finger, but it stayed lit. I pushed the LIFT OFF button, but nothing happened.

"We need some oil," Miles said. "I can't believe your father didn't top it off. How inconsiderate."

I looked at Miles like he was crazy, until he laughed. "Duh? Sandler? I'm kidding?"

"There's some fast food ahead," I said, pointing to an exit sign that had a spoon on it. "We can fill up there."

Miles started singing, "Fast food a-head, fast food be-hind, oh, we will never go-a hung-ry."

"You have a terrible voice," I said.

"I have a *great* voice," he said, aiming us off the high-way and into the parking lot of a Super Burger Barn.

"What's the difference between a Burger Barn and a Super Burger Barn?" I asked.

Miles shrugged. "About twelve bucks in neon?"

I walked in, past a huge plastic Cabbage Cow. Cabbage Cow was Burger Barn's mascot and spokesman. He wore a big apron and a chef's hat and handed candy to children at the end of a purple spatula. I could never understand why big smiley Cabbage Cow was so happy, given that most of his family had probably ended up between the seeded buns of a Triple Bac-O Burger. Shouldn't Cabbage Cow be in mourning? Shouldn't he have a black armband around his hoof? A black hoofband around his arm?

"Can I help you?" the counter guy asked.

"Yeah, can I talk to the manager?"

He looked scared. "Did I do something wrong? I greeted you, right? I was friendly, right?"

"No," I said, "you were great. You were perfect. This is about something completely different."

He looked relieved. He had a big button on his shirt with a picture of Cabbage Cow that said ASK ME ABOUT OPPORTUNITIES IN FRANCHISING!

"The manager's not here right now. The assistant manager is, but . . ."

"But what?"

"Umm . . . I dunno if talking to him is such a good idea. . . ."

"Why not?"

He looked down at the gleaming metallic counter. He looked up at the menu board. He chewed his bottom lip. He pulled at his hairnet and his bow tie and his hat. I felt sorry for him. "Okay," he finally said, and went into the back office. I could hear voices, and then a man walked out in a polyester outfit. It was Chad Chilton.

"Can I help you?"

The goatee was gone and he wore a tie and his hair was cut short, but it was definitely him. The counter guy was right. It *was* a bad idea. My entire body froze.

"Chad Chilton," I said.

He squinted, looking at me. "Yeah? Do I know you?"

'Umm . . . no . . . ," I said. "Definitely not."

"Okay, so? Andy here says there's a problem."

"No, no problem. . . . It's just . . ."

"Yeah?"

"Have you ever heard of bio-diesel?"

Miles pulled the van around back, by the kitchen door, and began unspooling the hose.

"Nice ride," Chad Chilton said, looking admiringly at the VW's spoiler. "Did you build this crazy thing?"

I wanted to say yes, but didn't. That would have been a lie. Not an exaggeration, a flat lie. I'd resolved that by the time we got to California, I was going to be different.

"Um, no. My father's a sort of inventor guy."

"Huh," Chad said, nodding, and then gave the cooks instructions on how to attach the onion ring machine to our pump. He spoke halfway decent Spanish. Then a clerk came out the back door. "Um, Cha . . . Mr. Chilton?"

"What is it, Ralph?"

"Someone wants to pay with their Cabbage Cow Gold Card, but the swipe thingy won't work."

Chad Chilton explained how to punch it in manually. Ralph sighed with relief and went back inside. Chad and I stood next to each other, shoulders practically touching, watching cars on the highway. Finally, I couldn't stand it anymore.

"You have no idea who I am, do you?"

"Excuse me?" he said.

"My name's Stan Smith."

He looked at me blankly. He adjusted his tie. I noticed he was wearing a nice watch.

"Stan Smith?" I said again. "We were in the same grade. A lot of the same classes, actually. Hey, I know what you'll remember. I lit your locker on fire."

He gave me a hard stare. I tensed up. Then he laughed. "*You're* the locker guy? Wow! That was some stunt."

"It was?"

"Hell, yeah," he said. "All my friends were jealous they hadn't thought of it first. You were, like, every pyro's hero."

"You're taking it pretty well," I said, "considering your stuff burned and all. Your leather jacket or books or whatever."

He shook his head. "No, I never use a locker. I just said that for the insurance. Some old junk burned. Actually, you did me a favor. They paid me almost three hundred bucks."

"And then after, you said you were going to kill me? Remember?"

He looked off into the distance. "No, I don't. I said that?"

"Yup."

"Huh."

He shrugged, and I believed him. I tried to remember. Was it possible I'd made it all up? I guess there weren't any real witnesses. Was it all a lack of *stifling creativity*? *Was I insane?*

Miles got out of the van. "Chad, *dude!*" he said. "What is going on?"

"Hey!" Chad Chilton said. "I remember this guy. . . . You're Niles, or whatever, right?"

"Miles."

"Yeah, yeah. Hey, are you still going out with that hot Cari chick?"

Miles looked at me, and then shrugged. "Umm . . . not really."

"Too bad, dude, she was hot."

"Yeah," Miles said, "except now she's busy being hot at college in Ohio."

"Not an easy distance, dude," Chad Chilton said. "Not good."

"Tell me about it."

The cook detached the hose. We were full. Andy the clerk ran outside and said, "Cha . . . I mean, Mr. Chilton! A bus of seniors just pulled up! They just ordered a hundred AARP burgers and extra Buzzy Fries and I don't even know how to ring the discount in!"

Chad looked at me and rolled his eyes. He rubbed his chin, where the goatee used to be.

"Anyway," I said, "it was good to see you."

"You, too."

He reached out to shake my hand. I took it. His was hard and leathery, but so was mine. A lifetime of scrubbing yams. Then Chad Chilton led Andy back into Super Burger Barn by the shoulder, explaining the register to him in slow, patient tones.

I looked at Miles. "Nice guy, huh?"

Miles punched me on the arm, really hard. I knew I deserved it. We got into the van and pulled onto the highway. He put some Led Zeppelin in the CD player and cranked it on full blast. I floored it, revving the engine to our maximum fifty-three miles per hour, and then swung the wheel, aiming straight for California.

"When we get there, I'm starting a band," he said.

"But you can't sing."

"It's going to be called Seeing For Miles."

"It's going to be called a lot of things," I said. "Mostly by angry audiences."

"You'll see," he said.

I leaned forward and turned up the radio, all the way to eleven, as we drifted into the fast lane.

Treatment for the feature-length film titled
GOING NOWHERE FASTER©
Written by Stan "Stan Smith" Smith

Okay, there's this one guy, see, and he's got an esteem problem. And doesn't have a girlfriend. And doesn't shave yet. And
his mom is an Amazon and his dad couldn't get a job at Ronco
if he paid them, and his house is, like, the pirate ride at
Disney World, and his sister is getting so old it's scary, and
his dog produces a tofu by-product that smells like a
thousand moldy bagels, and someone is trying to kill him.
Okay, that's your setup. Add a best friend who gets punched
in the nose and a kiss in a room full of bratwurst and a
quick trip to jail and a trashed store and a boss who could
eat his way to the moon without even trying, and you've got
what we call "plot arc." Then what happens is, these two guys
overcome all these obstacles, flat tires and painted dolls
and liar girls who will smooch anyone with lips and fat
hippie killers and, mostly, a complete and utter lack of
overall coolness, and they decide to hit the road, like get
in the world's coolest fry-burning van and drive across
vast, sprawling, virgin (don't tell anyone) America. During
this trip they find adventure, love, and the meaning of
life. It's a short film with a happy ending. It's a short
script with a great chance of being sold. Or maybe it isn't.
Maybe it's a horror story starring Jamie Lee Curtis. Or a
bunch of stapled paper with way too many commas. Either
way, these two guys are going to get great gas mileage. Or
whatever.

Going Nowhere

Who ever said all plots are a cliché? And what happens when you realize your boring life isn't as boring as you thought? And even if it is, what're the odds there's a whole lot more interesting material just over the state line?

"Here comes the state line!" Miles said.

I gave it 2 to 1 odds. I just needed a new title.

"How about *Dude, Where's My Scar?*" Miles suggested.

"How about *Drive, He Said,*" I said.

Cut to close-up, steering wheel. Cut to long shot, road. Cue music. Cue sound effects. Medium shot, van speeding. Close-up, yellow highway stripes blurring together. Off camera, laughing. Off camera, a tooting of the horn, beep-beep. Long shot, horizon, blue and still and welcoming in the celluloid distance.

Appendix

English Report
By Stan Smith
Mrs. Brompton's Class
4th Period

Stan—See me after class!

(F)

The Role of the "Teen Movie" in the Promotion of Hyper-Infantilism and the Subsequent Diminishment of Reality in the Modern Adolescent

It's a recent phenomenon. Some scientists have been referring to it quietly, and off the record, as "Mad Keanu Disease" (MKD). It typically starts with a sense of euphoria and renewal of hope among a certain type of dispossessed adolescent. Said adolescent watches a film about street dancers or Rollerbladers or competition surfers, who also happen to be good-looking fifteen-year-olds (disturbingly played by actors in their mid-to-late twenties), and as these actors overcome unlikely filmic obstacles, the gullible teen suffering from MKD becomes convinced that small cinematic victories can be applied to their own insurmountable problems. The MKD sufferer then returns to school thinking the Hot Girl might actually see beneath his nerdish persona and love him for who he really is, or the Football Player might be dissuaded from beating him to death through the timely usage of a clever phrase, or the correct combination of keystrokes and the spilling of a Jolt cola into the back of a computer might cause a crazy surge of CGI electricity that will turn his Dell into a talking-robot buddy and maybe even summon a beautiful model-servant who needs to be taught to dress herself.

Sadly, the outcome of these Teen Movie delusions usually involves, at the very least, further ostracism, but more likely a bloody sweater and a visit to the school nurse.

Other common sicknesses include: ***The New Kid in Town Syndrome***, in which being sort of different and funny and wearing a torn Clash t-shirt makes all the kids at the new school sort of like and grudgingly respect you after a few months of threatening you, especially when that girl you've been smiling at in English class turns out to be the girlfriend of the school's biggest bully. ***The Last-Minute Display of Talent Syndrome*** involves spending a few hours (in film time) being hassled and made fun of and caught up in nutty hijinks, like being tripped in the cafeteria or stuffed into a garbage can and rolled down the hill, and then being counseled by your friendly uncle or the sorta-crazy town mortician so when there's a big crisis, you suddenly display this hidden ability, like being able to fly an airplane or draw really well or perform a liver transplant or run really fast, and then everyone loves you.

Then there's the ***Swan Lie***, where you're this sorta mousy girl, even though everyone in the audience can tell you're actually pretty hot but are just wearing big bulky glasses and dumb clothes and no makeup, and then somehow you get into an argument with the hot girls in school, and then the funny-cool mom in town shows you how to dress and walk and wear eye-shadow in a heartwarming montage set to an old Journey song, and then you show up at the dance and amaze everyone by how hot you really were all along. The gym teacher almost comically swallows his whistle and the dumpy English teacher smiles with a tear in her eye, and when the football player comes over and wants to dance, you reach for the hand of your quirky but sensitive friend instead, the music swelling as you stare into one another's eyes in the middle of a joyously clapping circle.

Finally, and perhaps worst of all, is the ***Boy from Across the Tracks*** tale. See, there's a rich girl. And she has clueless (but not mean) rich parents and rich (but mean)

Appendix A

friends and a rich (total jerk) blond boyfriend, and yet, amazingly, she's not entirely happy. Despite owning a brand-new red Jeep, there's something missing in her life. Until that fateful moment when she first sees the Boy from Across the Tracks. He's usually working at an auto repair shop or a deli. Or maybe he's just the quirky punk-rock kid who hates everyone at school. Anyway, he and Rich Girl bump into one another, at first disgusted, but there's no denying the SPARK. They meet again somewhere, a few weeks later, like behind the pool house at some party, and realize they are PERFECT for each other. Her friends make fun of her, and his friends (if he has any) make fun of him, and then there's some misunderstanding that keeps them apart until the end of the movie, when they get back together, flouting all conventions of class and social expectation and audience gag reflex.

And so, it is these artifices (artifi? artificum?) and all their variations (really not that many) that have transformed much of current unpopular teen-dom into Unrealistic Fantasists, who, despite repeatedly using the above techniques in difficult situations and failing just as badly as they did in any situation previously, continue to be blinded by the maddening pink cloud of MKD. They continue to think that their funny pal "Booger" can teach them how to be alterna-cool by belching loudly and wearing goofy hats, or their mastery of "hacking techniques" can change their grades in the guidance counselor's office computer, or their clever use of a fishing rod and paper-clip hook can remove any number of hot cheerleader bras. It is a dangerous and deluded precedent set by the meat factory that is Teen Hollywood, and only with parental vigilance, toll-free hotlines, and many, many well-written pamphlets, can MKD be defeated.

Donate now.

Stan Smith's *Totally Official* List of the Sixteen BEST Truly Awful Films Ever Made
(Compiled somewhere between Nebraska and Utah)

ROADHOUSE — I don't think there's any question this tops
the list of the most hilarious two hours of moronic
genius in celluloid history. See, there's a roadhouse bar
outside of town, full of bikers who are just way too much
for one bouncer to handle. Or are they? Patrick Swayze, a
freelance bouncer/troubleshooter, is called in to restore
order, and quickly mops the floor with dozens of wild-
swinging henchmen, bringing them to their knees with
FBI-style finger-locks and snappy one-liners. Who knew
there was a professional bouncer's circuit? Who knew only
one man could be the best?

POINT BREAK — Best line: "It's death on a stick out there,
mate." The Swayze returns as "Bodhi," which is either
short for "Boddhisatva" or "Body Odor." In this role, he's
a Kerouac–style loner who can both surf *and* quote some
Yeats by the driftwood fire. Thing is, he *understands the
waves.* Keanu plays FBI agent "Johnny Utah," who goes
undercover to infiltrate Swayze's crew of bank robbers,
mostly by saying "Whoa" a lot and wearing sandals. Anthony
Kiedis from Red Hot Chili Peppers bounces around like
tattooed wallpaper to add street cred. Keanu almost gets
a face full of lawn mower. Almost.

THE POSTMAN — Kev Costner rebounds from *WATERWORLD*
in possibly the dumbest movie ever made. There's been a
nuclear holocaust, the government has collapsed, there's
no electricity or running water, but *someone* has to
deliver the mail, don't they? You bet they do. Kev wears

a leather trench coat and bravely hauls a bag of AOL
sign-up CDs, pizza menus, and offers for platinum credit
cards to survivor encampments, each one equipped with a
beautiful little rosy-cheeked girl wearing a torn and
muddy dress who stares with reverence as Kev roars off
on the best horse in all of Apocalypse-ville. The bad guy
has *a really thick* goatee and shows off some super-high
kicks that Kev handles with the old forearm-block. Men
ride horses *fast* in all directions. The decision to go
ahead and make this film, despite what had to have been
massive internal studio objections, rivals Mussolini's
green-lighting the invasion of Ethiopia.

SHOWGIRLS — It's possible this is just plain good.

TANGO AND CASH — Sly Stallone and Kurt Russell in a meeting
of the minds so unexpected that it seems possible, even
a half hour in, that this is really a documentary about
the Potsdam Conference. How did one camera manage to
shoehorn both egos into the same movie? Did they use a
special NASA lens? Anyway, somehow Sly and Kurt end up
in prison, where they beat up every single prisoner, twice.

COBRA — Sly (a loner cop named "Cobretti") blows away two
gang members while they're robbing the meat counter
of the local grocery store. "The only thing that stands
between these animals and the Black Forest ham is me!"

THE COLOR OF NIGHT — Includes many unpleasant shots
of a half-naked Bruce Willis. The script may have been
dictated by a transplanted brain being kept alive in a
jar of saline solution while being prodded by a series of
low-voltage electric shocks.

Appendix B

RAW DEAL – Arnold before both *THE TERMINATOR* and elocution school. Arnold drives a convertible Cadillac full-speed into a dump truck and walks away without a scratch on him. Arnold beats up a mannequin. Arnold has tiny handgun that somehow, instead of the usual eight, appears to hold a couple hundred bullets. He works his way up from mob enforcer to trusted confidant in order to exact revenge on the Big Boss, and then shoots 173 people. He somehow keeps a straight face the entire film, even though his character's name is "Joey."

THE SUBSTITUTE 2 – "I hate to say this, buddy, but I don't think detention is going to *do it* anymore." Treat Williams plays a substitute high school teacher who was in Vietnam, so he knows how to punch hard *and* employ the Montessori method. The school is full of bad types (graffiti, switchblades, torn spandex), and Treat puts up with them for about a day and a half, before deciding to take the whole package up a notch, mostly by replacing Thursday's meat loaf with knuckle sandwich on the cafeteria menu.

STONE COLD – Classic biker movie starring former NFL washout Brian Bosworth, who is pumped so full of steroids he looks like a balloon filled with lumpy gravy. The terrific Lance Henriksen plays "Chains," the head of the local biker gang. Big, expensive motorcycles get revved a lot, and then the Boz kills about 9,000 bikers. Later, he saves the world from drugs.

COCKTAIL – Tommy Cruise as a *hotshot bartender* on the national *bar circuit.* Tommy flips bottles of rum in the air and catches them behind his back. He pours many drinks

at once. He handles security *and* the register. The girls
are impressed. A subplot involves Tommy feeling bad about
the tough-but-honest waitress back home that he treated
badly while on his way up the bartending ladder. In fact,
he feels so bad about it, he stays in his dark apartment
and doesn't throw a bottle of rum in the air for, like,
three days. Rumor is they almost named this film *Citizen
Gin*.

TOP GUN — Stars Tommy Cruise, Val Kilmer, and the bald guy
from *ER*. Lots of Really Fast Motorcycles and Really Fast
Planes. Lots of bad mustaches. Lots of gender-confused
buttocks-kneading. Everyone has a nickname, like "Goose"
or "Maverick." In the end, the Russians lose.

ST. ELMO'S FIRE — All you need to know is that Rob Lowe
plays a sax player. (Oddly, his fingers aren't moving
but somehow lots of notes keep coming out.) Also, earnest
career sad sack Andrew McCarthy plays a tortured poet
(He's got writer's block? Maybe a haircut would help). Pre-
enhancement Demi Moore plays a world-weary party girl
who wants to go straight, but sadly invested too much in a
yellow Jeep. Pre-*MIGHTY DUCKS* Emelio Estevez plays pre-
MIGHTY DUCKS Emelio Estevez with the kind of style and
élan not seen since the robot from *SHORT CIRCUIT* tried to
learn how to dance.

BREAKDOWN — We all know that America's highways are
crawling with big, fat, mean killer truckers. It's in the
news every day. You've heard the stories. Big, Fat, Mean
Killer Truckers abduct people's wives and hide them in
their hundred-thousand-dollar underground lairs, and
then steal all the stuff in their wallets and cars. It's
like a goldmine. I mean, why bother actually driving a

load of tomatoes somewhere and getting paid for it, when you can kidnap someone's wife and then STEAL everything in their SUV? There's gotta be, like, eighty bucks in travelers' checks alone? Not to mention a socket set and three flares. But who would have thought they'd be dumb enough to pick on Kurt Russell? Anyone with half a brain knows Kurt's gonna give at least *one hundred and ten percent* to get his wife back. At least. Those are bad odds even for Big, Fat, Mean Killer Truckers.

HARLEY DAVIDSON AND THE MARLBORO MAN — Stars Mickey Rourke and Don Johnson. Isn't that enough? Voted #1 on the list of favorite movies by The Society of the Aggressively Dim.

GLITTER — Mariah Carey plays a younger version of herself by wearing her hair in two pigtails, and then later in the movie, not wearing them. She has a record producer/ boyfriend named "Dice." He wears a necklace dangling in his chest-hair through the whole movie that says "Dice." In the end, Mariah dumps Dice and then makes a lot of money with a combination of surgery and dance singles. Her boyfriend's name is Dice.